The
Break
of Dawn

ADVANCE PRAISE FOR THE BOOK

'The revolt of 1857 is a momentous event in the history of British rule in India. The people of a very large part of north India took up arms to throw out the rule of the *firangi*. Sepoys, drawn from the peasantry of north India, especially south-eastern Awadh, openly defied and killed British officers and their families; the sepoys were joined by the peasants to attack and destroy all that represented British rule. For leadership, sepoys and peasants turned to those who had been in authority before the arrival of British rule—the Mughal Badhshah, princes/kings/queens of regional principalities and to large taluqdars. It was in Awadh that this revolt against British rule became most popular and intense. This rebellion has been the subject of scholarly attention and debate, but the events have not drawn too much literary attention in terms of novels, plays, etc. It is thus good to read this novel and to have it in translation. Many of the principal participants of the revolt in Awadh are characters in this novel, which moves very swiftly over complex events. The register of the novel is distinctively nationalist. I am not sure if this novel is one of its kind. There could be similar narratives in Urdu or Hindi in existence. If this is indeed the case, then scholars like my young friend Dr Ali Khan Mahmudabad should make the effort to bring them before a wider reading public. I would like to end this note with a word of warning even if it sounds obvious: This is a work of fiction and thus everything in it should not be taken as fact. The imaginary is not history'—Rudrangshu Mukherjee, chancellor and professor of history, Ashoka University

'Sometimes, a book of fiction, an utterly readable and absorbing story that makes no claim to be a literary masterpiece, can open up doors to understanding that the virtuosity of a grand epic may fail to manage. *Aghaaz-e-Sahar* or *The Break of Dawn* is one such book. We could have easily passed it by; not known of its existence. However, we would have not known then that a page-turning and commissioned novel from 1957 such as this, written by a hardly known writer, tells us so much about our past, and by extension, the present. *The Break of Dawn* is historical fiction and embodies, as this genre always does, an imagination of the past. Unconstrained, unlike a historian, the fiction writer Khan Mahboob Tarzi invents (not that historians don't) a moment in the history of 1857 and imbues it with high romance and action. In the interstices of this history and romance, also lies an important story of the Hindu and Muslim joint participation in the rebellion of 1857. *The Break of Dawn* unearths a lesser known and acknowledged history, and employs the allegory of love that tells the tale of races and communities in one of India's most formative period . . . The novel's journey from Urdu to English has been steered by a bilingual writer and historian, who is most ably suited to undertake this task. That being said, the book in hand reads like a delightful bestseller, and not an intellectual task. This is its most remarkable achievement'—Rita Kothari, translator, writer, and professor of English, Ashoka University

The Break *of* Dawn

KHAN MAHBOOB TARZI

Translated from the Urdu by
ALI KHAN MAHMUDABAD

VINTAGE
An imprint of Penguin Random House

VINTAGE

USA | Canada | UK | Ireland | Australia
New Zealand | India | South Africa | China

Vintage is part of the Penguin Random House group of companies
whose addresses can be found at global.penguinrandomhouse.com

Published by Penguin Random House India Pvt. Ltd
7th Floor, Infinity Tower C, DLF Cyber City,
Gurgaon 122 002, Haryana, India

Penguin
Random House
India

First published in Vintage by Penguin Random House India 2021

English translation copyright © Ali Khan Mahmudabad 2021

Illustrations by Labonie Roy

ISBN 9780670093618

Typeset in Bembo Std by Manipal Technologies Limited, Manipal
Printed at Replika Press Pvt. Ltd, India

www.penguin.co.in

MIX
Paper from
responsible sources
FSC® C016779

To my father, a patriot and a worthy inheritor of
Muqeem-ud-Daula, who has tirelessly waged
a different kind of battle for his rights

—*Ali Khan Mahmudabad*

Contents

Introduction   xi

A Note on the Illustrations   xxxiii

Author's Preface   xxxvii

1. The Kindness of the Mutineers   1
2. A Show of Loyalty   13
3. The First Message   25
4. Arrest   38
5. Set Free   51
6. The Confabulations   62
7. A Time of Loyalty   76
8. A Conference between Three Leaders   88
9. Unrest in the Residency   100
10. Alice under Suspicion   111
11. The Battle of Ismailganj   124

12. The Crowning of Birjees Qadr   136

13. The Struggle   149

14. Bloody Warfronts   162

15. The Advance of Hope Grant   175

16. The Wisdom of Maulvi Ahmadullah Shah   187

17. Alone in the Desert   200

18. The Last Proclamation   212

Acknowledgements   229

Introduction

'Abba, why is it called Muqeem Manzil?'

I was not more than ten or eleven years old when I asked my father this question. Muqeem Manzil was the part of our home in Mahmudabad that was reserved for formal occasions. As children, we were only allowed to go there under supervision. Of course, there was some trepidation in going there alone anyway because people used to whisper about how some of the rooms were now occupied by *jinns* and also the ghosts of those who had been killed in the *ghadr*—the so-called 'mutiny' or rebellion of 1857.

My father responded saying that the place was named Muqeem Manzil after my great-great-great-grandfather, Muqeem-ud-Daula Raja Nawab Ali Khan, who had died fighting against the British in 1857.

'Is there a painting of Muqeem-ud-Daula, Abba?'

My father replied that there was no painting, but family lore has it that he looked like my grandfather, was short in

stature and had a full face with a pink complexion. He was
an accomplished poet and a student of Wajid Ali Shah. His
poetry survives to this day. However, all other historical
records were either lost, destroyed or had fallen victim to
armies of termites. My father added that Sartaj Ali Khan
'Chabban', who looked after my brother and I, was from
a place called Chatauni, near which Muqeem-ud-Daula
had died.

Having escorted Begum Hazrat Mahal to Nepal, he
was in Seota when he heard that the Qila of Mahmudabad
had been destroyed by the British. He swore that he would
not step foot in an area which the British had taken over.
A few days later he passed away from his battle wounds in
Seota. Before his passing, he had willed that he be buried
in the replica of the shrine of Karbala that he had built in
Mahmudabad. His grave is still in the shrine. An allusion
to his decision to stay in Seota and his desire to be laid to
rest in the shrine can be found at the end of his *Diwan* or
collected works of poetry, which were put together by his
son, Amir-ud-Daula. In fact, the title of this novel, *Aghaaz-
e-Sahar*, contains within it an allusion to Muqeem-ud-
Daula. *Sahar* means dawn and 'Sahar' was also his *takhallus*,
or nom de plume, which he used when he composed Urdu
poetry. One day at the shrine, my father mentioned that that
there was an Urdu novel written about 1857 in which the
protagonist was a soldier from the armies of Mahmudabad.
I asked if he had a copy, and he asked me to check with the
librarian.

One of the few primary sources that exist about
Muqeem-ud-Daula are the diaries of Colonel W.H.

Sleeman, who toured Awadh between 1848–50. On 19 February 1850, Sleeman met 'Nawab Allee', as he called him, and wrote:

> On reaching camp, I met, for the first time, the great landholder, Nawab Allee, of Mahmoodabad. In appearance, he is a quiet gentlemanly man, of middle age and stature. He keeps his lands in the finest possible state of tillage, however objectionable the means by which he acquires them.

Sleeman's accounts of both Bilehra, a collateral branch of the Mahmudabad family, and Mahmudabad paint the Rajas as fierce and wily land barons who used all possible means to expand their holdings. Naturally, family lore has it differently. Many uncles bemoaned the fact that it was rich of Sleeman to pass judgement against the zamindars and taluqdars when he was part of a government that had colonized vast tracts of land and subjugated entire races in different continents. The truth was probably something in between for it was, and indeed remains, impossible to build up large estates and fortunes without being somewhat ruthless and calculating. On the other hand, Sleeman's disdain for both the Hindu and Muslim rulers of the area comes through in his diary entries and perhaps is an indication that his observations reflect his own prejudices. Sleeman says to Nawab Ali Khan in Lakhpeda, an orchard of a 1,00,000 mango trees, that,

> Sheikh Sadee, the [Persian] poet, so deservedly beloved by you all, old and young Hindoos and Mahommedans, says, 'The man who leaves behind him in any place, a bridge,

> a well, a church, or a caravansera, never dies.' Here not
> even a respectable dwelling-house is to be seen, much less
> a bridge, a church, or a caravansera.

Nawab Ali Khan replied that it was safest not to invest
wealth in things that could be destroyed.

Sleeman then asked whether the landlords were aware
of the loans offered by the British government, to which
Bakhtawar Singh, a zamindar who was travelling with
him, replied that people who live in the countryside know
nothing of the government paper (the loan document) and
only people in the cities understood its value. In any case,
the landlords and peasants wouldn't know how to keep the
papers safe, let alone understand how to take advantage
of the government schemes and when to draw on their
interest. Indeed, it was the fear that Hindu and Muslim
landholders had of the threat to their cultural, economic,
political, religious and social ways of life that was in part
responsible for sparking the uprisings of 1857.

Many historians have demonstrated that one of the
causes of the 1857 uprisings was the fear both Hindu and
Muslim landlords had of the changes the British had made in
land revenue collection. The doctrine of lapse and direction
annexation both caused widespread uproar. The former
was used to usurp the lands of rulers without heirs and the
latter was invoked to annex lands by claiming they were
badly administered. Awadh was annexed in 1856 by Lord
Dalhousie, which led to the kingdom becoming a hotbed
of discontent. Apart from protecting their own interests, the
landlords were also joined by common people who feared the

increasing influence of Christianity and perceived a threat to their culture and way of life. This was aided by rumours that gun cartridges were greased using pig and cow fat, which, in turn, caused discontent among underpaid Indian soldiers serving the British. Perhaps the uprisings failed precisely because they were not truly an organized and collective effort at resistance but a confluence of various interests that were not tied together through a united leadership. Begum Hazrat Mahal of Awadh and Emperor Bahadur Shah Zafar, the last Mughal ruler, were both no more than figureheads, and this paved the way for the British to institute direct rule. After the uprisings, Muqeem-ud-Daula's son, Amir-ud-Daula Raja Mohammad Amir Hasan Khan, who was still an infant when his father was killed, was installed as the raja by the British in a show of 'Christian magnanimity and charity'.

My brother used to often remark about how strange it was that across the courtyard from Muqeem Manzil, in another part of our house called Tedhi Koti—befitting perhaps—there hung two portraits of Queen Victoria and King Edward VII. Often, bureaucrats, officers and politicians would come and marvel at the portraits but then ask why they weren't taken down and put away. The answer that I heard most often was that this too was a part of history, whether we liked it or not, and so there was no use in hiding such things away. It was better to understand what happened and come to terms with the past, its complexities and contradictions, rather than try to hide them. As a child, however, I did always secretly wonder what Muqeem-ud-Daula would have made of these portraits since his entire

Qila had been demolished by the British in retaliation for his participation in the events of 1857. As children, once we heard that the British had been responsible for his death, my brother and I used to sometimes go and stand in front of the portraits of the British monarchs and stick our tongues out at them and make faces. Naturally, Queen Victoria remained unmoved by our impudence.

Perhaps being exposed to these contradictions of history, albeit through objects, places, people and their memory, tempered my view about how to relate to the past. I grew up in the 1980s in India, and the uprisings of 1857 were often discussed in my family by the elders as they sought to understand their own family history and, consequently, the establishment of British rule. Elderly aunts often spoke of how the trauma of 1857 was never forgotten by Amir-ud-Daula, who grieved his entire life and felt embarrassed at the manner in which Mahmudabad had survived, because of the 'magnanimity' and 'Christian charity' of British administrators and officials. They spoke of how this trauma was passed down the generations. Some relatives thought that the house in which we lived in Lucknow had seen too much bloodshed, and worried about how that might affect those who still live there.

Qaiserbagh was looted by Punjabi, Scottish and Gurkha soldiers who had arrived as reinforcements in Lucknow. In fact, I only managed to see some of the looted treasures of Lucknow when there was an exhibition at the Musée Guimet in Paris. Apart from objects and manuscripts on loan from the Queen of England's collection, there was also a beautiful photographic exhibition in which Antonio

Martinelli had tried to recreate photographs taken by Felice Beato in the aftermath of 1857. Although there is debate about how Beato staged photos of the corpses, they nonetheless provide a graphic reminder of the vengeful fury of the British. Perhaps the only other record that evokes similar if not even more pronounced feelings is the poetry written during or in the aftermath of the uprisings.

My father would on occasion recite a couplet, attributed to Bahadur Shah Zafar, that spoke of the decline that the advent of the British heralded in his mind. No doubt many of these couplets were the vehicles through which the distant memory of 1857 was passed down to him through his elders.

> *Yeh ri'aaya-e-hind tabah hui kahoon kaisi in pa jafa hui*
> *Jise deikha hakim-e-waqt ne kaha yeh bhi qabil-e-daar hai*
> *Yeh sitam kisi ne bhi hai suna k di phaansi lakhon ko begunah*
> *Val-e-kalma goyon ki samt se abhi dil men inke ghubar hai*

(These people of India have been destroyed, what can I say of their suffering
Whoever the rulers lay eyes on is destined for the gallows
Has anyone heard of this injustice, that so many were sent to be hanged
Indeed, they bear a grudge in their heart against those who declare their faith)

We would often remark on how the last line, despite having been written in a different age and context, resonates with today's atmosphere in which Indian Muslims feel targeted on the basis of their religious identity. The term 'kalma-go' is a reference to Muslims as those who have recited the *shahada* or declaration of faith: 'There is no God but Allah, and Mohammad is his messenger.'

At other times, my father would recite this couplet by Ghalib:

Hindostan saaya-e-gul paaya-e-takht tha
Jaah-o-jalaal-e-ahd-e-visaal-e-butaan na pooch

(India was sheltered by flower petals, a pillar of the divine throne
Don't speak of the epoch of the arrival of the haughty idolators)

In school at La Martinière College in Lucknow, we were taught that 1857 was the first national war for independence. No one questioned what was national about it and what kind of independence the rebels strove for. Some years later, in school in England, some of the textbooks spoke about the atrocities of the mutineers, and occasionally one of the older teachers would speak of the great blessing that the British Empire had been in bringing civilization to those parts of the globe that had not been illuminated by the light of the Enlightenment. As with all nationalisms, the fact that Hindus and Muslims had come together to oppose the British was used as the foundation stone for building the edifice of secular nationalism in independent India.

Historians debated whether this was accurate or not for the reasons mentioned above, but nonetheless, in the popular imagination it became the moment in which the seeds were sown for liberation from British rule. The bloody and horrific images of the aftermath of the revolt, with 'mutineers' being tied to cannons and blasted to bits, became seared in people's minds. In the build-up to Independence, many Indians wrote of 1857 as the watershed moment in the history of the freedom movement. Even V.D. Savarkar, the ideological progenitor of Hindutva, wrote approvingly of the communal cooperation between Hindus and Muslims in 1857 against the British. Of course, the ends to which he sought to use this were entirely different from those envisioned by the members of the Congress Party and others, who used 1857 as a building block for constructing a pluralistic and secular Indian nationalism.

Interestingly, even after Independence, the appropriation of 1857 by the Congress Party to argue for a secular nationalism was contested by Hindu revivalists. By this time, Savarkar had also radically changed his position and argued that the most important and consistent divide in Indian history was that of Hindus and Muslims.* According to declassified police intelligence reports from 1955, there were a series of high-profile meetings of members of the Hindu Mahasabha, the Ram Raj Parishad, the Rashtriya Swayamsevak Sangh and its political wing, the Bharatiya Jana Sangh.

---

* D. Ludden, *Making India Hindu: Religion, Community and the Politics of Democracy* (Oxford: Oxford University Press, 1996). Also see C. Jaffrelot (ed.), *Hindu Nationalism: A Reader* (New Delhi: Permanent Black, 2009). For Savarkar's own views, see V.D. Savarkar, *Hindutva* (New Delhi: Hindi Sahitya Sadan, 2003).

A confidential report written by the superintendent of police, Special Branch, Criminal Investigation Department, Patna, noted:

> One of the leaders said that 1657, 1757, 1857 are famous for mutiny in the history of India, and therefore a mutiny must come in 1957. He openly said that Ram Rajya will be established in 1857 [read 1957] but not that Ram Rajya which was dreamt of by Mahatma Gandhi. Staunch Hindus will be the rulers of this Ram Rajya.*

The report further linked the designs and plans of the 'evil elements of these communalists' to the riots that took place in Calcutta, Bihar and Uttar Pradesh. Of course, there was no mutiny in 1957, but on the other hand, the government organized grand centenary celebrations that sought to commemorate 1857. As Rudrangshu Mukherjee notes, initially, Jawaharlal Nehru was somewhat critical of the failure of 1857 as being a 'feudal outburst' in *The Discovery of India*, which was written in Ahmadnagar Fort between 1942–45. However, a decade later, as Nehru stood up in Ramlila Ground in Delhi to celebrate the centenary of 1857, he spoke of it as the 'First War of Independence' and glossed over the earlier analysis of it as a military uprising

---

* D. Jha, 'To Mark the Centenary of 1857, Gau-Rakshaks Planned a "Mutiny" in 1957', Scroll, 25 April 2017, last accessed, 11 March 2021, https://scroll.in/article/834787/to-mark-the-centenary-of-1857-gau-rakshaks-planned-a-mutiny-in-1957

that was a last-ditch effort by the feudals to remain relevant and protect their interests.★

As part of this effort to memorialize 1857 as evidence of the first stirrings of nationalist awakening, the government commissioned a scholarly work of history, which was written by Surendra Nath Sen. The government also brought out a rather badly produced book, entitled *1857: A Pictorial Presentation*. The same year, R.C. Majumdar published *The Sepoy Mutiny and the Revolt of 1857*, and S.B. Chaudhari published *Civil Rebellion in the Indian Mutinies (1857–59)*. These three books provided the historical foundation stones for subsequent scholarship on 1857 and its role in India's nascent nationalism. Away from the Marxist, imperial, nationalist and post-colonial debates about the nature of 1857, popular culture also aided the memorialization of the events in the public's consciousness.

In 1946, just before Independence, a film entitled *1857* was made by Mohan Sinha for Murari films, which did very well at the box office. In the same year, the writer Vrindavanlal Varma published a novel called *Jhansi Ki Rani Laxmi Bai*, and Niyaz Fatehpuri published a drama entitled *Jhansi Ki Rani*. Before Independence, 1857 had become a leitmotif for a number of plays, novels and poetry across India. Namakkal Ramalingam Pillai published poetry in Tamil in 1924, only for it to be proscribed by the British. A number of Sikh and Hindu authors wrote poetry and prose

★ R. Mukherjee, 'Two Responses to 1857 in the Centenary Year', *Economic and Political Weekly*, 43, no. 24, 2008, pp. 51–55, last accessed 11 March 2021, http://www.jstor.org/stable/40277566

in Punjabi, and published the compilation under the title
Ghadr Ki Goonj, some of which was subsequently published
in the Gurmukhi script in the *Ghadr* newspaper based in
San Francisco. Ramanlal Basantlal Desai published *Bharelo
Agni* in Gujarati in 1935; long ballads were composed in
Telugu by poets like A. Venkataratnam; A. Ramamurty
published *Viplava-1857* in Kannada; Vasant Varkhedkar
wrote *Sattavancha Senani* in Marathi; and Om Prakash
Sharma published *Saanjh Ka Suraj* to much acclaim in Hindi.
A poem about the Rani of Jhansi written by the Gandhian
poet Subhadri Kumari Chauhan became extremely popular.
I remember in school we memorized whole stanzas from it,
and the line '*khoob ladi mardani, woh to Jhansi wali rani thi* (she
fought like a man, she was the queen of Jhansi)' would be
recited as soon as her name was uttered.

Despite the relative dearth of literature and poetry about
1857 in various Indian languages, in Urdu there is wealth of
material going back to the period. Notwithstanding historical
analyses and commentaries that sought to critically engage
with the events of 1857, like Syed Ahmad Khan's *Asbab-e-
Baghwat-e Hind*, figures like Bahadur Shah Zafar, Asadullah
Khan 'Ghalib', Sadruddin 'Azurda', Hakim Mohammad Taqi
'Sozan', Hakim Agha Jan 'Aish' Dehlavi, Lala Ram Prasad
'Zahir', Zahiruddin 'Zahir', Syed Mehdi Hussain 'Mehdi',
Mirza Sachche Sahib 'Mehr', Mirza Baqir Ali Khan 'Kamil'
and Hafiz Ghulam Dastgir among others composed poetry
on the calamitous events of 1857. Many used the genre of
shahr ashob, the lament or affliction of the city, in order to
mourn the destruction and violence wreaked by the British.
An anthology of these shahr ashob about 1857 was published

in 1863 by Tafazzul Husain 'Kaukab'. Interestingly, a lot of those poems were disparaging of the rebels and dismissed them on the basis of their purportedly lower class and caste backgrounds.* In 1888, Deputy Nazir Ahmad published a novel called *Ibnul Waqt*, and subsequently, in the twentieth century, Khwaja Hasan Nizami wrote a number of novels about 1857, including *Begamat ke Aanso* (1924), which went into thirteen reprints by 1942. Rashid Ahmad Jafari wrote a novel entitled *Ghadr*, and Rashidul Khairi wrote *Naubat-e-Panja Roz Ya Vida-e-Zafar*.

By the time of the centenary celebrations of 1957, a number of books had been commissioned, and one of those was this novel, *Aghaaz-e-Sahar* (*The Break of Dawn*), by Khan Mahboob Tarzi. Tarzi was living in Lucknow at the time and was part of a group of authors who were writing prose, short stories, novellas, novels and dramas at a prolific pace. Unfortunately, much of this has not been studied sufficiently as Lucknow has always been associated with, and researched, as a centre of poetry. Indeed, there was no serious engagement with Tarzi's life and works until Dr Umair Manzar published a book in Urdu in December 2020, entitled *Khan Mahboob Tarzi—A Popular Novelist from Lucknow*.†

---

* For more on this genre and in particular on Kaukab's *Fughan-e-Dehli*: Soofia Siddique, *Remembering the Revolt of 1857: Contrapuntal Formations in Indian Literature and History*, PhD thesis, School of Oriental and African Studies, 2012, last accessed online 11 March 2021, https://eprints.soas.ac.uk/13540/1/Siddique_3333.pdf

† Umair Manzar, *Khan Mahboob Tarzi: Lucknow Ka Ek Maqbool Novel Nigar* (Lucknow: Nomani Printing Press, 2020).

Khan Mahboob Tarzi was born in 1910 in Hussainganj but eventually came to be known as a veritable living example of Lucknow's famous culture. The only exception was his insistence throughout his life on wearing a tie and a suit on almost a daily basis. His initial schooling was at the Wesley Mission School and then at the Amiruddaula Islamia College. He obtained his BSc from Aligarh Muslim University. His interest in writing began at university and his son Khan Masood Tarzi writes that his stories were published in *Nairang-e-Khayal*, *Mahnama-e-Saqi* and *Alamgir*. In Aligarh he was a supervisor at a lock-making factory, and thereafter he became a store clerk in the army. He also tried his hand at directing and film-making, and did a stint at a studio in Calcutta and then at dramatization with R.S. Bhargav. For a while he worked with the Lucknow radio station and then was transferred to Delhi. He was in the army until 1943. Between 1934 and 1958, he was a regular writer for *Sarpanch*, which was published by Nasim Anhonavi, who ran the Naseem Book Depot. In those days, many publishers would ask novelists to write on demand and there were a number of novelists like Tarzi who did this, such as Wahshi Mahmudabadi, Nadim Sitapuri and Ziya Azimabadi. Naseem Book Depot also published the works of Wasl Bilgrami, Shaukat Thanvi and Ma'il Malihabadi.

Although Tarzi tried his hand at journalism, his heart lay in writing novels. According to various estimates, he wrote and published more than a hundred novels. His subjects were varied and included romances, mystery and detective novels,★ historical,† social‡ and political novels, and as Shamsur Rahman Faruqi writes in his preface to Umair Manzar's book, Tarzi was probably one of the earliest science fiction writers in Urdu.§ Throughout his life, Tarzi faced financial hardships, though he gratefully accepted what publishers paid him for his work. Another son, Khan Rashid Tarzi, went so far as to write that publishers had sucked the very lifeblood out of his father, and being the honourable man that he was, he slaved away for pennies. In 1958, owing to a large family and burgeoning responsibilities, he left Naseem Book Depot and tried his hand at being a freelance novelist. In fact, this novel was published by Idara-e-Forogh-e-Urdu in Lucknow and was printed by Sarfaraz Qaumi Press. It was initially sold for Rs 8. Interestingly, the publishers mentioned that in Karachi it would be available at Anwar Book Depot in Empress Market in the Sadar area, which shows that Tarzi's books had a readership in Pakistan. By the time Tarzi was writing this novel, he had become weak from stress and the pressures of making ends meet.

His son Khan Masood Tarzi writes that almost eight years before his death in 1960, his father had become a

---

★ Some of Tarzi's detective novels are *Paigham-e-Ajal*, *Turpai* and *Gorakhdhandha*.

† Some historical novels he wrote include *Subh-e-Andalus*, *Nawab Qudsiya Mahal*, *Nazuk Ada Begum*, *Qamar Tal'at*, *Jaanbaz* and *Muqaddas Lahu*.

‡ On Awadhi life and culture, he wrote *Awadh Ke Baanke*, *Rassi Jal Gai*, *Dulhan*, *Aminabad*, *Sailaab* and *Anjuman* among others.

§ Some of his science fiction novels include *Safar-e-Zohra*, *Barq Paash*, *Do Diwane*, *Ek Jaan Teen Qalib*, *Udan Tashtari*, *Mehr Afroz*, *Masnoo'i Chand* and *Tilism-e-Hayat*.

gaunt figure, both because of his worries and responsibilities but also because he was constantly working and writing. The children had to forgo school for lack of money, and at home there was often nothing to eat. Tarzi, however, continued to work and write, almost as if driven by a madness, while his children wondered why he worked so hard when his pay was not even that of a third-grade clerk. But writing was never merely a profession for him. Khan Rashid Tarzi writes that his father would often say, 'Writing for me is like worship, and one does not expect to be paid for worship.' In order to earn a little extra money, Tarzi wrote some erotica under the pseudonym Wahi Wahanvi, but, as Shamur Rahman Faruqi writes in his preface to Manzar's book, what was regarded as lewd, obscene or erotic literature at that time would be harmless compared to what is produced today.

Tarzi wrote a number of historical novels about 1857, including *Aghaaz-e-Sahar*. Published in 1957 on the centenary of 1857, it is a work of historical fiction, but many of the protagonists in this novel were real historical figures whose involvement in the uprisings of 1857 are well documented by historians. *The Break of Dawn* is a much simpler novel than Ruskin Bond's *A Flight of Pigeons,* which was made into the film *Junoon* by Shyam Benegal. Curiously, the two novels—*The Break of Dawn* was published twenty-one years before *A Flight of Pigeons*—have similar protagonists. Tarzi's novel features Alice, a young English girl, and Riyaz Khan, a young soldier from the rebel army. Tarzi relied on a number of official histories and British gazetteers for his information, and thus was an unconscious part of a later historical method that sought to read into the colonial archives what the rebels were planning and thinking. The novel is fast-paced, although it does try to convey the manner in which Hindus and Muslims not only lived and worked but also fought side by side. Interestingly, the main theme of the novel is a romance between the young English girl and the rebel army soldier. Most of Tarzi's characters are from the upper castes and *ashraf*, and they all speak Hindustani, although those from the qasbas would have also spoken various rural dialects, including Awadhi among each other.

As I mentioned earlier, I had first heard about Tarzi's novel from my father when I was searching for more information about Muqeem-ud-Daula. Having searched for a copy for years in vain, I had forgotten about this novel. However, in 2017, I was reminded of *Aghaaz-e-Sahar* when a number of politicians stood up in Parliament while trying to justify a bill they were passing and spoke about how my family had been traitors for having sided with the British in 1857. I vividly remember recoiling in rage as I heard these words on television and decided that I would try and find the novel and translate it, as a small, even insignificant way, of paying homage to my ancestor, Muqeem-ud-Daula.

A few weeks later, I was going through our library and the manuscript collection, and chanced upon a copy of the novel. I set about translating it straight away. Of course, the novel is a work of fiction but nonetheless, it is also a record of a time during which the memory of 1857 was being used to conceive of and build a pluralistic and harmonious idea of India. As Rudrangshu Mukherjee has said, this novel is firmly of the nationalist genre and it is important to remember that 'the imaginary is not history'. However, it is also important to remember that the processes and ideas of imagining the nation are equally important, and it is precisely when the work of imagining a harmonious nation is neglected that extreme, rigid, myopic and jaundiced ideas prevail. Therefore, the idea of India that this novel imagines continues to be historically instructive because the model of religious and social harmony that it sought to portray as an ideal sixty-four years ago is now being replaced by intolerance, divisiveness and prejudice.

The stories that we tell of our pasts also shape our future. I recall that as a child I had often heard that the Hindu rajas of Ramnagar Dhamedi were our blood brothers and that the pact went back to an oath sworn between Muqeem-ud-Daula and Raja Guru Baksh Singh in 1857 to fight the British. Both of them are mentioned in this novel. Eventually the families went their separate ways, and we lost touch with each other. However, I happened to reconnect with Rajkumari Anshika Singh from the current generation of the Ramnagar Dhamedi family last year, on Mahmudabad's Instagram page of all places. I had posted something about translating this novel and had also mentioned that the rajas of Ramnagar Dhamedi were our blood brothers. I couldn't contain my joy when she also narrated that she had been told as a child that our ancestors were blood brothers. Rajkumari Anshika Singh wrote, 'I was told that they participated in [a] blood oath of sorts, slicing open their palms to mingle their blood as a mark of fealty and fraternity. The blood of the covenant is thicker than the water of the womb.' Stories make us who we are.

Though not of high literary merit perhaps, *Aghaaz-e-Sahar* is a simple yet beautiful fictional snapshot of what William Dalrymple called 'a human event of extraordinary, tragic and often capricious outcomes'.★ For me, translating this novel was a chance to pay homage to Muqeem-ud-Daula, who died escorting Begum Hazrat Mahal to safety in Nepal, and to Khan Mahboob Tarzi, a hitherto largely ignored novelist whose work deserves to reach a wider audience. I hope that more of his other novels, some of which have been mentioned above, are translated and published.

A Note on the Translation

The novel is written in a fast-paced style in simple and colloquial Urdu. I have endeavored to leave in as few Urdu words as possible, except when the context requires the original in order to convey meanings that might otherwise be lost in translation. I have left *firang* and *angrez* untranslated but have translated *gora* as 'whitey', as I find that the English word is perhaps more forceful in conveying the pejorative way in which it was used. All the footnotes in the chapters are Tarzi's original footnotes, except for the ones marked 'Translator's note'. One of the joys of translation is becoming intimately familiar with the world that a text evokes. However, one of the difficulties of translating certain words is that they no longer remain embedded in

---

★ W. Dalrymple, *The Last Mughal: The Fall of a Dynasty: Delhi, 1857* (New Delhi: Penguin, 2007).

the sociocultural and religious matrices from which they emerge. For instance, the food stalls set up by Muqeem-ud-Daula for Muslim soldiers were called *bawarchikhanas* and the ones set up for Hindu soldiers were called *bhandaras*. The use of these words immediately evokes the primacy of religious feeling among people from different communities, and although there was much camaraderie between Hindus and Muslims, there was at the same time a strict adherence to the religious injunctions about comportment as well as eating and drinking. This did not detract from the deep-seated friendships that existed despite these differences in personal piety.

In independent India, this camaraderie and bonhomie was often called *Ganga–Jamuni tehzeeb* or sometimes called 'composite culture'. Unfortunately, this label came to imply a harmony brought about by the dilution of religious practice and orthodoxy, and connoted a compact between members of class and caste elites. In truth, however, our ability to live together separately was the result of our having deep and sincere roots in religious traditions. Today, the increasing divisions between people from different communities is perhaps the result of our being caught in a kind of schizophrenia between modernity and tradition. On the one hand religious practice in an increasingly interconnected world has become more performative, while on the other hand it has also become somewhat detached from its deeper roots. The causes for this are more than can be done justice to in this brief note, but suffice it to say that this has to do with the other frameworks that we all necessarily inhabit today in one way or the other, all of which partly shape our identities: globalization, the emergence of the nation state as the dominant form of political representation, industrialization, urbanization and, of course, the rise of the virtual world of the Internet and social media. One logical concomitant of this are changes in the language, in the broadest sense, spoken by communities. Words undergo transformations of meanings, new vocabularies are created and indeed, with the rise of technology the very grammar and syntax of language change. Therefore, novels such as *Aghaaz-e-Sahar* become even more important, as they provide a snapshot of the time and place in which they were written and the audiences for whom they were intended.

Ali Khan Mahmudabad

A Note on the Illustrations

Illustrating this book was a challenging and exciting process. While reading the text for the first time, I got the opportunity to visit Lucknow, thanks to the translator, Ali Khan. I visited the Residency, Mahmudabad Qila and many other places mentioned in the book. It felt surreal to be present in the very spaces the characters (and historical figures) in the book lived. As I stood in front of the Residency of Lucknow, I could visualize how the walls crumbled under fire. At the Qila, I could hear the hooves of the rebels' horses galloping through the courtyard. These visceral experiences felt like an overlap of times, spaces and cultures.

I wanted the visuals to complement the layers within the narrative, and to this end I was influenced by two very different artistic styles. The history books I had read while growing up represented Lucknow, Delhi, Meerut and other sites of the mutiny, through black-and-white photos by European photographers. These were supplemented by grand oil paintings and intricate etchings by British artists for newspapers and humour magazines, like *Punch*, that were published in the United Kingdom. These images relied on visual realism and scale to represent the power and might of the British Empire. They contrast heavily with Indian court artists' representation of royalty—beautifully detailed and delicate miniature paintings of Mughal kings and nawabs. These paintings tell their story through stylized two-dimensional figures, fantastical elements like halos, and create a graphic representation of reality. This visual dichotomy seemed integral to the telling of the story, and posed an exciting challenge: How could I combine the two distinct narratives of realism and stylistic visuals into a cohesive style?

As a mixed-media artist, I love nothing more than experimenting with different materials. After some trial and error, I was able to create a visual language that combined my influences through physical and digital collage. Each character from the book is rendered as a moveable paper puppet dressed in tailor's scraps, and was photographed and edited on to the scenery created from photos and paper cutting. This allowed me to replicate detailed characters across illustrations in different moods and movements, while preserving the stillness and staccato body language common to the photographs and miniature paintings of the time.

Past and present photographs of Mahmudabad Qila, courtesy of the Mahmudabad Estate, feature heavily throughout the book, alongside pictures of Lucknow from the nineteenth century and present day. For example, in the illustration where Riyaz ferries Begum Hazrat Mahal across the river, the image of Musabagh in the background is a photograph by Felice Beato from 1858. Each illustration involved hours of historical and geographical research, the result of which was a desk covered in cloth, paper and wire scraps as I pieced the artworks together.

I hope the illustrations offer several more layers for you to dip into as you are transported to Lucknow from a very different time.

Labonie Roy

Author's Preface

The Break of Dawn recounts tales of a time when Indians awoke from their deep slumber and united against the British. They did so without caring about the differences of sect or faith, in order to secure their freedom. The fight spread to every corner of north India, including present-day Uttar Pradesh, and led to some of the bloodiest events in the history of the subcontinent. The Indians fought against the British and their supporters with the greatest conviction. In Awadh, not only the soldiers but the common people also took up arms. They all went to battle under the leadership of the taluqdars as well as of others.

Among those who fought and died to free us from the yoke of the British was the taluqdar of Mahmudabad, Raja Nawab Ali Khan. Raja Guru Bakhsh Singh of Ramnagar Dhamedi was one of the leaders who participated in the Siege of Lucknow, while the armies of Raja Loni Singh of Mithauli and the army of Mahmudabad were at the forefront of the fight.

The deeds and struggles of Raja Nawab Ali Khan in the First War of Independence are some of the greatest from the period. In this novel, I have written about a few of his services. This martyr of the freedom movement took up arms against the British, tried to foil their devious plots and amassed a great army in order to defend Lucknow.

In Lucknow, the leaders and soldiers of the siege made Nawab Ali Khan their general. He was at the front, fighting along with his soldiers and organizing food and water for his troops as well as supplying them with arms.

He organized *bhandaaray* (food stalls) and shelters in and around Lucknow, where soldiers would be given free food and a place to rest. Nawab Ali Khan sacrificed everything he had for the freedom of the country. If all his services were to be collected and written about, a rich history would emerge.

In presenting the deeds of this martyr of the independence movement, the following books have been used:

i)   *The King's Mutiny in Awadh*
ii) *History of the Indian Mutiny*
iii) *Afzal ut-Tawarikh*
iv) *Ahsan ut-Tawarikh*
v)   *Lucknow and Sitapur Gazettes*

Bagh Aaina Bibi   Khan Mahboob Tarzi
Hussain Ganj, Lucknow
25 April 1957

1

The Kindness of the Mutineers

One by one the stars were disappearing, and the darkness of the night was slowly dissolving into the first rays of dawn. The breeze grew stronger and the birds began their morning song.

Riyaz yawned, turned over and tried to pull the sheet over his head when a man sleeping nearby gently nudged him and said, 'Riyaz, it's dawn. Won't you pray?'

Riyaz raised his head slightly, looked around and sat up. His colleagues were snoring and near the bushes, a group of eight to ten armed young men were standing, chatting with each other.

Riyaz rubbed his eyes, looked around once more and replied to the man, 'Bannay Khan? Amazing! Woke me up and now you're asleep again?'

'Riyaz Bhaiyya?' a man called out from under a tree. 'What's happening?'

'Nothing, Shukla Ji. I am just trying to wake Bannay Khan up.'

Riyaz got up, folded his bedding and took out a handkerchief from an earthen pot nearby, putting it on his shoulder. He picked up his rifle and placed it on the bedding. The noise had awoken a few others, and they were packing their belongings. Riyaz stood up with a yawn, put on his shoes and started walking towards the young armed sentries when someone called out, 'Riyaz Miyan, I am coming too!'

He ambled over to the sentries. Seeing him, one of them said, 'Don't go unarmed towards the river!'

'Yes, but you lot are here. Pandey Bhaiyya?'

'Yes. Let's go. I'll come too.' Pandey took the rifle off his shoulders and said, 'There are a lot of wolves and jackals here.'

Both men chatted with each other and strolled towards the river, clearing a path through the bushes. There was a light mist hovering above the river and thousands of herons were near the bank.

Riyaz turned to his companion and said, 'What do you say, Laxman Pandey? I just want to spread my bedding and go back to sleep here.'

'Why don't you pray? Then you can sleep. Anyway, we shall be moving on by afternoon.'

'Yes, but one shouldn't sleep after morning prayers.'

'That's true. Anyway, those who wake up early live longer,' Laxman Pandey said as he walked with Riyaz. 'Rahman Chacha also used to say this. In any case, you go wash up and I shall stand over here.'

Riyaz walked into the shallows. Meanwhile, another eight to ten people arrived, greeted Laxman Pandey and walked to the river. A little later, Riyaz came out of the river and, rubbing his face with a towel, asked Laxman Pandey, 'Did Maulvi Karamat Ali also come?'

'Yes, he came after you left. Look, here he comes,' he said, pointing towards the river.

Maulvi Sahib was hurrying along the path next to the river. Climbing to the top of a sandbank, he said, 'The sand is cool at this hour.'

'Yes, Maulvi Sahib,' Riyaz replied. 'But after a few hours it shall become so hot that you could roast chickpeas on it.'

'Yes, Riyaz Miyan. The loo will blow today. This cool breeze will become hotter than an oven in the afternoon.'

People were coming and going. Maulvi Sahib looked towards the east and said, 'We are losing time. We shouldn't wait for more people.'

Everyone prayed on the banks of the river and returned to the camp in small groups. Some people were still lying around snoring. A middle-aged man called out to Riyaz, 'The head of the mounted police has called for you. I would have told you last night but you were already asleep and I didn't want to wake you.'

'When did you meet him?' asked Riyaz.

'Before sunset, in that village, where we stopped to eat.'

'So are they camped somewhere close by?'

'Yes, there is an orchard near the village where 200 men from the second platoon and 100 men from the forty-first are camped.'

'Good. I'll go there now because he promised to give me Colonel Birch's horse.* That horse is actually mine. A couple of months ago, I had sold it to that *firangi* to raise some money for my sister's wedding. Now Maulvi Sahib has saved it as war booty and will return it to me.'

'Go, then. There is some time before breakfast but you can eat there, and hurry back!'

Riyaz went back to his bed, picked up his rifle and, pointing at his belongings, said, 'If I am late, load my things with the others.'

He strapped his rifle on to his back and, walking along the edge of the bushes, set off towards the north. After about half a mile, he saw eight armed men. They all belonged to his platoon and were standing in the bushes, looking in the direction of the river. He walked towards them and asked, 'What's the matter, Bachcha Singh?'

'There's prey . . . prey,' he whispered.

'Is it a deer?' asked Riyaz.

'Yes, three deer and four stags. Just near the reed bushes.'

Riyaz looked towards the river, where Bachcha Singh was pointing, and, without thinking, he exclaimed, 'Huh?'

Near the reeds, there stood three firangi women and four firangi men, glancing around nervously. The men were carrying rifles. One of Bachcha Singh's companions growled, 'Let's get them from here.'

---

* Colonel Birch was the commander of the 41st Indian Army (technically 41st Regiment of the Native Infantry) in Sitapur. On 3 June 1857, the soldiers mutinied and looted the treasury. Colonel Birch was killed in front of the treasury. His wife and daughter fled to Lucknow with some others.

'Not now,' said an old man. 'We don't have long-range rifles. Let them get nearer. They will come this way.'

Riyaz shuffled around for a better view. He stared for a while and said, 'They are not soldiers.'

'Yes,' Bachcha Singh said, 'I think they are coming from Muhammadi or Shahjahanpur. It would be better to arrest them.'

The rest of the soldiers watched them silently. The English were now away from the reeds, walking slowly on the sandbank, towards the trees. The old man started to raise his barrel but Riyaz forced it down, saying, 'They are trying to save themselves. Besides, there are women with them.'

'So what?' Jarakhun rebutted. 'The day before, a company from the 41st killed twenty-five to thirty Englishmen in Muhammadi and Shahjahanpur. There were women there too.'

'I know. Kirpal Singh was there and he told me everything,' Riyaz retorted to the old man. 'We are soldiers and we can only engage with soldiers. Just yesterday we swore before the major that we would only fight those who attack us.'

A young soldier interrupted, 'But they are armed and if we were in front of them, they would have shot at us.'

Riyaz replied, 'Surround the trees and ask them to surrender. If they don't drop their weapons, kill them.'

'That's a good plan. We can easily surround them from three sides.'

'All right,' Jarakhun replied, 'You all go this way and I will go with Beeka, Nanhu and Ramzan Khan towards the other side.'

The three soldiers and Jarakhun hurried off and disappeared into the bushes.

The English were crossing the highest point of the sandbank. Six armed men with loaded rifles stood around Riyaz. One of them said, 'What are we waiting for now? Let's move.'

The Englishmen were moving forward carefully, and the women were following them.

Riyaz turned towards the river and was about to speak when a rifle shot rang out from where the English were. They turned to see who had fired the shot. Riyaz jumped out on to the sandbank and fired another shot in the air. The English were shocked and quickly turned to go the other way. The rest of the soldiers had joined Riyaz and were peering down the barrels of their guns.

The Englishmen froze and Riyaz shouted to his companions, 'They'll drop their weapons. Don't fire!'

Jarakhun and his three soldiers had looped around and were standing on a different bank. Riyaz motioned to the Englishmen, 'Put your weapons on the ground!'

He started moving towards them as Jarakhun and his companions drew in from the other side. The Englishmen hadn't put down their weapons, and Riyaz and his men were edging closer to them.

Riyaz shouted again. 'I said, put your rifles down on the ground!'

The Englishmen looked at each other. Their faces were white as a sheet. The women were trembling from head to foot. One of the women spoke to the others nervously and the men put their rifles on the ground.

Riyaz said loudly, 'Stay where you are and put your hands in the air!' The English had their hands raised in plain sight as Riyaz and his men walked up to them. One of the soldiers picked up the Englishmen's rifles and slung them across his shoulders. Riyaz stood silently, sizing them up.

None of the four men were from Sitapur; three were old and one was younger. Two women were middle-aged, while the third was about eighteen. They were all staring at Riyaz with nervous, pleading eyes. Seeing their condition, Riyaz's anger subsided and he felt sorry for them. Just a few days earlier, he and his companions had to defer to them and address them as superiors.

In a friendly voice, he said to them, 'Where are you coming from?'

'From Muhammadi,' replied one of the Englishmen.

By now, Jarakhun and his companions had also got close. Jarakhun said to Riyaz, 'Let's search these people and take whatever they have.'

'No, we have no right to search these people,' Riyaz commanded him. 'Subedar Sahib will come in a short while, and we shall hand these people over to him. If he thinks that they should be searched, then so be it.'

Jarakhun was left speechless. Riyaz was meant to go and meet the Risaldar Sahib about getting his horse back, but after seeing the attitude of Jarakhun and a couple of other soldiers, he had changed his mind and decided that his horse could wait. He led the Englishmen and women towards the rest of his companions, who lay hidden in the woods. At the sight of the English prisoners, they all gathered around them and started speaking to each other. Upon seeing the pretty young Englishwoman, one of the soldiers said to another, 'Bhagawati, it seems God has answered your prayers.'

Riyaz flew into a rage. 'Lalta Singh, how dare you utter such words? You should be ashamed of yourself.'

Lalta started laughing to hide his embarrassment.

Another soldier interjected, 'Lalta, you have behaved in this despicable manner before, and it does not befit a soldier to stoop to such base levels.'

'Shukla Ji, I was just joking . . .'

'What kind of a joke is this, with those who are in our custody and depend on your mercy?' Riyaz said to Lalta. 'These antics will only cause us to stray from our goal.'

'Riyaz Ahmad Khan, you are right,' said Shukla Ji. 'There are a few bad apples in our company who are forever talking of looting and killing. We should tell Subedar Sahib about these problems.'

Jarakhun looked at Shukla Ji; he then bent his neck and stared at his own feet. Riyaz made the prisoners sit under a tree. He turned towards Shukla Ji and another soldier and said, 'Watch over the prisoners. I am going to go and retrieve my horse.'

'Okay, Riyaz Miyan, you carry on,' said Shukla as he slung his rifle over his shoulder. 'We will keep an eye on them.'

Riyaz left, and Shukla Ji deployed fifteen armed guards around the prisoners and sat under another tree, leaning on his rifle. Other soldiers dispersed to find shade as well. Jarakhun wandered over to Shukla Ji and said, 'Shukla Ji, this young blaggard is trying to order us about. I shall ask Subedar Sahib to tell him to watch himself.'

Shukla Ji stared at Jarakhun for a moment. 'There is no need to get upset, Jarakhun. Riyaz might be young but he is upright and courageous, and it is because of these qualities that everyone has started respecting him.'

'I respect him too,' said Jarakhun. 'But now he is trying to boss us around and I don't agree with this.'

'You're wrong,' said Shukla Ji. 'He is not one of those young men. You probably misadvised him and he didn't listen. That is why you are upset.'

Someone shouted from a distance, 'Subedar Sahib is coming!'

The soldiers stood to attention and saluted the subedar. He dismounted from his horse and looked at the prisoners. Shukla Ji stepped forward and said, 'Riyaz has just arrested them near the river.'

Jarakhun interrupted. 'Riyaz only got here later. We spotted them first, hidden in the bushes near the bank.'

'Well, I am glad that Riyaz also reached there,' said the subedar. 'Otherwise you lot would have probably killed these unfortunate wretches. In Sitapur you killed civilians, and that saddened me.'

Jarakhun was lost for words. The subedar went up to the prisoners and spoke to them briefly before stepping aside to stand under the shade of a tree. Shukla Ji went up to him and asked, 'What are your orders with regard to the prisoners?'

'We will release them. Firstly, they are not soldiers. And secondly, they are accompanied by women.'

'They seem very tired to me.'

'Yes, they have been following the banks of the Sarayan all night, and they haven't eaten anything for two days.'

Shukla Ji replied, 'Our breakfast is coming. So we can share that with them. After that, if you think it appropriate, we can set them free. Oh, and they had rifles, which we impounded.'

The subedar thought for a minute and said, 'Another company of military police are camped two *kos*★ away from here. They are under Jamadar Harpal Singh and Rajab Ali is also with them. If they find these prisoners they won't spare them.'

'So what should we do?' asked Shukla Ji.

'First let them eat something.'

Soon after Shukla Ji left, eight to ten soldiers brought breakfast in some pots. Shukla Ji offered *poori*s, sweets and milk to the prisoners, and then distributed everything among the soldiers. The subedar wandered over to the thickets, and by the time he returned, everyone had finished their breakfast; they were all sitting in small groups. Riyaz had also returned and was standing next to his horse, talking to Shukla Ji and Maulvi Karamat Ali.

The subedar had temporarily put those three officers in charge and had told every soldier in the company that they must obey their orders. He sat under a huge tree and motioned them to come over.

'The sun is getting stronger, so I suggest you take the prisoners to some nearby village, where they won't be harmed. They can leave for Lucknow at night.'

★ Translator's note: Kos is a unit of measurement from ancient India and is approximately equivalent to three kilometres. In many parts of rural north India it is still used to measure distances.

Riyaz said, 'Towards the south-east, about one-and-a-half kos from here, there is a village called Mankapur. The villagers will give them refuge, and if there is a spare bullock cart, they may even take them to Lucknow.'

'Take them to Mankapur,' said the subedar, 'and take fifteen soldiers with you.'

Riyaz replied with a salute. He then turned to Shukla Ji and said, 'I am leaving my horse here, please look after it for me.'

The subedar interjected, 'If the women can ride, horses can be arranged. There are already two horses here, and one can come from the neighbouring village.'

Riyaz, Shukla Ji and the maulvi liked this suggestion. Riyaz asked the English if the women could ride. And then one of the villagers, who had come with the breakfast, brought a horse from his village.

Riyaz helped the ladies on to the horses. Presently, the English prisoners and the fifteen soldiers set off for Mankapur.

2

A Show of Loyalty

Mankapur was one and a half kos south-east of Sarayan River. Riyaz and his men could have reached in less than an hour, but they decided to stop and rest in an orchard. The Englishwomen couldn't carry on because of their thirst, and so Riyaz turned to one of his companions, Jawahar Singh, and said, 'Thakur, find these people some water from the well in the orchard. Otherwise they might get heatstroke.'[*]

'Yes, Riyaz Bhaiyya, this girl looks like she is already getting worse.'

Entering the orchard, Riyaz turned to one of his companions and said, 'Bhaiyya Ganga Din, take out your pot and rope and fetch these people some water.'

---

[*] Translator's note: The original expression used by Riyaz is, '*Loo lag jayegi.*' The loo is a particular kind of hot wind that blows during the summer and is held to be very bad for one's bones and health in general. It is also regarded as indispensable for a good mango crop.

Ganga Din obeyed him. Riyaz and his companions drank their fill as well and were about to leave when twenty riders and a Hindustani officer confronted them. Riyaz and his soldiers saluted the officer and stood to attention. The officer responded to their greeting and asked, 'Where are you taking these foreigners?'

'Mankapur,' Riyaz said, stepping forward. 'We found them by the banks of the Sarayan. We are escorting them to Mankapur, from where they will be taken to Lucknow.'

'They will neither go to Mankapur nor to Lucknow,' the officer spat out. 'We will take them to Adamabad.'

Riyaz nervously stared back at the officer. The Englishmen and women had also begun to tremble. Jawahar Singh stepped forward and said, 'No, sir. We have granted them refuge.'

'I am telling you, they'll be killed in that orchard,' replied the officer in a commanding voice. His face was beginning to show his displeasure at this insolence, and his eyes grew bloodshot.

Riyaz, getting equally worked up, said, 'We have granted them refuge.'

'Soldier, you are overstepping yourself,' said the officer angrily. 'What is your name?'

'Riyaz Ahmad Khan.'

'My name is Dulha Khan. I am ordering you to hand them over to me.'

'You are not our commanding officer,' replied Riyaz.

'I am an officer in the army, and you are nothing but a common soldier,' said Dulha Khan. 'You have to obey my orders.'

'Each army is free now,' replied Jawahar Singh. 'And we have made Raja Nawab Ali Khan our leader. He has ordered that English children, women and non-combatant men not be killed. They should be safely escorted outside district lines.'

'I am not bound by his orders.'

'Neither are we bound by yours,' Riyaz countered.

Furious, the officer levelled his rifle. Riyaz and his companions also shouldered their rifles.

Dulha Khan said, 'Look, don't make this worse. I don't want to harm people who are on my side.'

'I can say the same to you,' replied Riyaz. 'We can only win our independence if we adhere to our principles, sir.'

'What do you want?' asked Dulha Khan in a calmer voice.

Confidently, Riyaz replied, 'Only time will tell what we want. These Englishwomen are in our custody and we shall safely escort them to Mankapur.'

Another soldier from the officer's company said to Dulha Khan, 'Let's move on, otherwise we will fall far behind the others.'

'You have insulted me today, soldier,' said Dulha Khan. 'I shall not forget this.'

Riyaz grew angry again and said threateningly, 'If this matter can be resolved by combat, then so be it. I am ready.'

Dulha Khan's brow furrowed, and in a contemptuous tone he asked, 'You dare challenge me to a duel?'

'Yes,' Riyaz shot back. 'My forebears always settled matters of honour in this way.'

One of Dulha Khan's officers stepped between the two and said, 'This is not the time for personal duels. Let's hurry, because we will not be able to catch up with them.'

'All right. Soldier, if I live, then I am sure our paths will cross very soon.' Dulha Khan slung his rifle on his shoulder and brought his horse closer to Riyaz. 'Remember, my name is Dulha Khan.'

'And my name is Riyaz Ahmad Khan.'

Jawahar Singh and his companions had formed a circle around the English to protect them. Dulha Khan and his soldiers had left the orchard, but Riyaz and his companions kept their rifles levelled until the band disappeared from sight.

Jawahar Singh said, 'Are they from the Mallawan cantonment?'

'They can be from anywhere,' Riyaz retorted. 'If the matter had become too heated, I can promise you there would have been bodies everywhere.'

'Riyaz Ahmad Khan!' the old Englishman tried to get his attention. 'This is the second time you have saved our lives. God will protect your life and have mercy upon you.' His accent was like that of the other Englishmen, but he spoke polished Urdu. One of the ladies said something in English, which the young girl translated for Riyaz, 'We are all grateful to you and your companions.'

'We are just doing our duty,' replied Riyaz to the young girl. 'We are fighting against the Company, not against you.'

'Come on, Bhaiyya Riyaz, let's move,' interjected Jawahar Singh, 'We must not linger around here anymore. They might come back with an entire force and surround us.'

They left the orchard and went into the fields. Riyaz, Jawahar Singh and Ganga Din were walking in the front. Behind them were the women on horseback, followed by the Englishmen on foot, and then the rest of the soldiers.

The gusts of the loo were becoming fiercer. Riyaz, Jawahar Singh and Ganga Din took off their turbans and gave them to the Englishwomen so they could protect their faces from the sun. After about a mile, they stopped to rest and drink water from a nearby well. A small group of farmers was sitting under the shade of a tree near the well, eating roasted chickpeas. One of them had a basket filled with about forty or fifty snake cucumbers.* Riyaz bought the entire lot for four annas and, giving the English two pieces each, distributed the rest among his companions. They continued their journey and shortly arrived in the Mankapur district.

The zamindar of Mankapur, Ram Tirath Pandey, lived in the centre of the village, in a magnificent haveli. He was sitting in council at a *chaupal*† in front of his haveli with some farmers. As soon as he saw the Englishmen accompanied by soldiers, he stood up and squinted to get a better look. Riyaz and Jawahar Singh greeted him, bringing their horses to a halt next to the chaupal.

Ram Tirath Pandey turned to the farmers and said, 'Go and fetch eight to ten charpoys!'

---

* Armenian cucumber, also known as *kakdi*. It has a thicker skin, is thinner and longer than a cucumber.
† Outdoor thatch-roofed area to sit in.

Riyaz, Jawahar Singh and Ganga Din were still standing in the sun, holding their horses' reins. On hearing Ram Tirath's voice, a couple of villagers came out of their houses and cottages. Ram Tirath called out to a few of them and said, 'Take the horses into the orchard, water them and give them some grass.'

By this point, Riyaz and Jawahar Singh had entered the chaupal. Riyaz turned to the Englishwomen and said, 'Please sit on the charpoys.'

Ram Tirath asked Riyaz, 'Bhaiyya, where are you all coming from?'

'Pandey Ji, have you not recognized me?' said Riyaz as he wiped the sweat from his forehead. 'I am Riyaz, son of Rustam Ali Khan, from Mahmudabad.'

'Oh, Riyaz Bhaiyya, it's you!' Ram Tirath said with astonishment. 'By God, I didn't recognize you in military clothes.' He embraced Riyaz and slapped him on the back, saying, 'I meet your father every couple of months, but I haven't seen you in ages.'

'Yes, Pandey Ji. It must have been about four years.'

Jawahar Singh bade the Englishmen sit on the charpoys, took the saafas from the women and put them on an empty charpoy. The other soldiers had made themselves comfortable on the floor. In the meantime, some villagers had brought a few more charpoys. Ram Tirath beckoned to them and said, 'Kidaar, go and make a few urns of sugarcane juice for our guests. Bijoo, tell Mutaee and Sarju to bring some water so that everyone can freshen up.'

Riyaz said to Ram Tirath, 'Pandey Ji, if you have some cool room in your haveli, perhaps the sahib *log* can go and sit there. They cannot stand this weather, you see.'

'You're right,' Ram Tirath replied. 'I am sorry I didn't think of it earlier. Let's go and sit in the underground chambers. I was going there anyway.'

Riyaz put his saafa on his head and said to the English, 'Come. You must be uncomfortable here.' They followed Riyaz towards the haveli while talking to each other in hushed tones.

Ram Tirath turned to the soldiers and said, 'Why don't you also come? What will you do here?' He led them all into a large room in the haveli.

Meanwhile, a couple of villagers brought urns full of sherbet and some *aabkhowras*.★ One of them addressed Ram Tirath, 'Pandey Ji, the water is also ready.'

The visitors washed their hands and faces, drank their fill of the sherbet and sat comfortably on the charpoys. Riyaz explained everything about the English to Ram Tirath.

'. . . and this is why Subedar Sahib especially sent me. He wanted me to request you to arrange for these people to be taken to Lucknow.'

'Don't worry, Riyaz Bhaiyya. By tonight I shall arrange for bullock carts, and these people shall safely reach Lucknow. Just the other day, I arranged for eight to ten ma'ams and their sons to be escorted to Lucknow. The chief commissioner even gave confirmation of their safe arrival. But, Riyaz Bhaiyya . . . But . . . never mind.'

He glanced over to the English and fell silent. He softly nudged Riyaz's leg, motioning him to come outside with him. Riyaz looked around and said, 'Jawahar Singh, you wait here. I'll be right back.' As he stood to step out with

---

★ Translator's note: *Aabkhowras* are clay cups.

Ram Tirath, he turned to the English and said, 'Why don't you get some rest? The soldiers will go to another room.'

'Yes, your excellencies. My house is not worthy enough for you,' said Ram Tirath sheepishly. 'But please let me know if you need anything.'

Jawahar Singh said, 'Pandey Ji, perhaps, if there is another room, the soldiers could get some rest too?'

Ram Tirath turned to Bijoo. 'Bijoo, take these people to the room next to the storeroom.'

The soldiers left with Bijoo, and Riyaz said to the women, 'You should also get some rest now.'

The English seemed slightly at ease as the young woman said to Riyaz, 'Mr Riyaz, we shall never forget you. You are an angel, not a human, and your companions are also good people.'

Riyaz was about to respond when Ram Tirath interjected, 'Memsaab, he is the son of a very important man and is very brave. Brave men always treat their enemies properly.'

The young woman turned towards Riyaz and then looked at the floor. Riyaz and Pandey left the room, stood under the shade and started talking to each other.

Ram Tirath said, 'Riyaz Bhaiyya, you are very generous. And why not? After all, you are your father's son! The old proverb is famous, "*Baapat poot, praapat ghoda, bahut nahin toh thoda thoda.*" The father's character is reflected in the son. But Bhaiyya, if you ask me, I would honestly say that giving these people shelter is asking for trouble. Just yesterday, my son Gopal returned from Lucknow. He said that about fifty men from some platoon from Sitapur escorted some Englishwomen and children to Lucknow.

On reaching there, the commander took the soldiers to Machchi Bhawan and asked them to lay down their arms. When they refused, he had them shot.'

'Pandey Ji, I have also heard this,' replied Riyaz. 'But my faith and my ancestors' ways tell me that we should always behave kindly and properly with our enemies. We shall fight those who fight us, but we must give shelter to those who ask for it.'

'You are right. This is why I had some Englishwomen and children escorted to Lucknow the day before yesterday.'

Riyaz narrated the incident from the orchard and said, 'If I hadn't been ready to fight that mounted company, they would have killed these people right there.'

'Bhaiyya, *bhagwan* will keep you safe and sound.'

After talking about this and that for a while, Riyaz said, 'Pandey Ji, I should take my leave now.'

'Let the afternoon mellow, then leave. Where will you go in this scorching heat?'

'Subedar Sahib asked me to return quickly. We might be returning to Mahmudabad today.'

'Your Raja Sahib is a great man,' said Ram Tirath. 'The day before yesterday, three of his soldiers escorted five Englishwomen and children to Lucknow, and last night, on their way back, they stopped here.'

'He is a diehard opponent of the firangis, but he hasn't yet caused harm to anyone. He has decided to come out and openly fight the English.'

Jawahar Singh stuck his head out the haveli door and shouted in their direction, 'Why don't you come and sleep for an hour or two?'

'I was planning to leave now, but Pandey Ji says I should leave in the evening.'

'I agree. It's too hot and the winds are too strong. The loo will make you ill. You rest. I am coming.'

Jawahar Singh went back inside the room. Riyaz resumed his conversation with Ram Tirath. After a while, Ram Tirath said, 'Look, you too take rest. I am going to have something cooked for you in the meanwhile.' Riyaz headed towards the haveli but paused for a moment and called out to Ram Tirath.

'Could you put a couple of people on guard duty?'

'Don't worry. I have already told Sarju.'

Ram Tirath disappeared through one of the doors of the haveli. Riyaz went into the room the soldiers were in and sat down on a charpoy. The rest of the men had fallen asleep. Only Jawahar Singh was awake, but he too was feeling drowsy.

Riyaz lay down close to him. After a few minutes, Jawahar Singh was fast asleep and snoring.

About half an hour later, one of the villagers peered into the room. Riyaz immediately sat up and asked him, 'What's the matter?'

'Pandey Ji has sent an urn of water.'

'Take the water to the sahib log's room.'

The villager stared at him, puzzled. Riyaz smiled and took the urn to the other room himself. The English were all fast asleep. He quietly placed the urn next to the door and was about to tiptoe back out when the young English girl called out to him softly. Riyaz looked at her and paused. She got up from her charpoy, walked towards him and gave him an innocent stare.

'Mr Riyaz!'

'Yes?'

'Are you planning to leave us now?' she asked, sounding sad.

'Yes, I am.'

She stared at him with pleading eyes and Riyaz's heart began to beat faster.

'Riyaz,' she exclaimed as she took his hands in hers and stared into his eyes. She tried to say something but couldn't find the words.

The firangi girl's touch had sent a tingle through Riyaz's body, and he nervously took a step back. The girl called out to him again in the same pleading tone.

Riyaz stuttered, 'Yes . . . you . . .'

'My name is Alice,' said the girl, with some difficulty.

One of the Englishwomen rolled over in her sleep. Alice retreated, and Riyaz hurried out of the room.

3

The First Message

Riyaz reached the shade of a big tree and called out for Jawahar Singh.

'What's the matter, Riyaz Bhaiyya?' Jawahar Singh asked as soon as he came out.

'Let's go. Everyone must be waiting for us.'

'Yes, it's useless to wait here any longer. Pandey Ji will safely escort those people to Lucknow.'

Jawahar Singh moved closer to him and said, 'Pandey Ji is near a bunch of banana trees and is coming this way.'

'Pandey Ji is preparing food for us, but it will be a hassle to carry it.'

Before Jawahar Singh could say anything, Pandey Ji arrived and asked, 'What's the matter? Why didn't you sleep? I already ordered the guards to be alert.'

'Pandey Ji, we'll take your leave now,' said Riyaz. 'Subedar Sahib must be waiting for us.'

'But Bhaiyya, I have had some food prepared for your journey. Why don't you wait a little longer?'

Riyaz apologized profusely, but when Ram Tirath Pandey would not accept any excuses, he said, 'All right, when we pass through here tonight, we will pick it up.'

Pandey Ji made him promise before allowing them to leave. Jawahar Singh called out to his companions, who emerged with rifles slung across their shoulders. Riyaz said, 'Pandey Ji, remember that the *firangs* are at our mercy. There are women with them, and we must look after them and keep them safe.'

'Bhaiyya, don't you worry,' said Pandey Ji. 'I will personally escort them to Lucknow.'

As Riyaz and his companions were about to set off, Alice came out of the haveli. The moment she saw that the men were ready to leave, she said something in English to the other firangs, and they came out as well. Pandey Ji, Riyaz and his companions all paused to look at her. Alice whispered something to her companions and then went to Riyaz and Pandey Ji.

'What's the matter, Miss Baba?' Pandey Ji asked Alice.

'I have come to thank these people.'

She looked at Riyaz with longing in her eyes and, without any hesitation, moved close to him and clasped his hands. 'Mr Riyaz, I would like to thank you once more on behalf of my companions and myself. We would like nothing more than to be taken to Lucknow by you and your men. But of course, we don't want to inconvenience you.'

The other English also came close to Alice, but she held on to Riyaz's hands and kept speaking. 'My name is Alice.

Alice Harrison. My elder brother, Major John Harrison, is in Lucknow. I was in Shahjahanpur with my younger brother, Philip Harrison, who left for Hardoi.'

'May God ensure your safe passage to Lucknow,' replied Riyaz. 'If there had been time and had circumstances permitted it, we would certainly have escorted you to Lucknow, but Pandey Ji will take you there.'

The Englishmen also thanked Riyaz and his men. Alice remained frozen in her place, gazing longingly at Riyaz's face. He said to her, 'Good. Now please permit us to be on our way.'

Alice leaned forward and kissed Riyaz's hands. He got flustered and nervous.

Alice let go of his hand and said, 'We are only alive because of you. May God reward and bless you for this.' She spoke in fluent Urdu.

Riyaz lifted his hand to say salaam.

'Khuda hafiz,' stuttered Alice, as if the words wouldn't come out.

Riyaz said salaam to Pandey Ji and went to the chaupal. Pandey Ji followed him. The men had already prepared the horses. After thanking Pandey Ji, they all left the basti.

Jawahar Singh said to Riyaz, 'Tell me, Riyaz Bhaiyya, can young girls from our homes speak to strangers like this?'

But before Riyaz could reply, a soldier shouted out, 'Speaking to strangers is one thing. This one kissed Riyaz Bhaiyya's hands!'

'Yes, Avtar Bhaiyya. I got very nervous. Even now I can hear my heart beating!'

Another soldier laughed and said, 'Well, she is very beautiful.'

Riyaz turned to him and smiled. They chatted and soon reached their companions. Some soldiers were on guard while the rest of them slept in the shade of the dense trees. The subedar, too, lay under a tree. As soon as he heard their voices, he sat up and beckoned to Riyaz.

'I just heard that Captain Forbes,★ along with some women and children, has left for Lucknow and that every cantonment's regiments are gathering near Nawabganj.'

'But we need to go to Mahmudabad. Raja Sahib is waiting for us.'

'Yes. That's why I have called for you. I am going to Hardayalpur. Three companies of our battalion have already reached there. I am going to ride there and you bring that company also.'

After explaining some other important things to Riyaz, the subedar went his way. An hour later, Riyaz woke everyone up, and they set off for Mankapur. Pandey Ji had had four horses loaded with water and food for the soldiers. In another two hours, they were in Hardayalpur.

Three companies from their battalions were waiting next to a lake near the basti. Everyone ate and rested, and at midnight they set off towards Mahmudabad.

Early in the morning, they met 300 soldiers who were on their way from Khiri and Muhammadi to Nawabganj. By late afternoon that same day, they arrived in the grounds

---

★ Captain Forbes, accompanied by cavalry and infantry, went to Sitapur to escort some English refugees to the safety of Lucknow.

in front of the Qila of Mahmudabad. Raja Sahib asked them to rest in one of the orchards and called for the subedar to confer with him.

Apart from Raja Sahib's special guards, around 2000 to 2500 locals had gathered there. They were all carrying swords, rifles and other weapons. The subedar emerged from the Qila after sunset. As soon as he reached the orchard, he sat down on the edge of a well and called for Riyaz, Jawahar Singh, Laxman Pandey, Shukla Ji and Maulvi Karamat Ali.

Maulvi Karamat Ali said, 'I have heard that Thakur Loni Singh has started corresponding with the British.'

'Yes, that is exactly what Raja Sahib was saying,' said the subedar. 'But the English won't help him as there are fifteen or twenty English refugees in his Qila, whom he wants to send to Lucknow.'

Laxman Pandey interjected. 'On reaching Lucknow, they will tell them everything about our movements, our location and our plans.'

Riyaz replied, 'You are right. But we shouldn't give them enough time for this. The fight will begin in Lucknow.'

Shukla Ji said, 'Before making any decision, we should send a man to Faizabad to ask Maulvi Sahib for his advice.'

The subedar replied, 'Raja Sahib thinks so as well. So tomorrow morning, we will send Jawahar Singh to Faizabad.'

Puzzled, Maulvi Karamat Ali asked, 'But he has been in the firangis' prison for the last month, hasn't he?'

'He should have been freed by now,' said the subedar, 'because it had been decided that as soon as we take up weapons, we would free Maulvi Ahmadullah Shah. The fact is that he is leading our War of Independence, and we will await his instructions.'

Jawahar Singh turned to the subedar and said, 'If you permit, I want to take two soldiers with me.'

'Of course,' replied the subedar. 'Lalta Singh and Shaikh Ahmad will go with you. Both are good riders.'

'Please instruct them now that we shall be leaving at four in the morning tomorrow.'

'Right, I shall tell them now,' replied the subedar. 'You go and rest.' At this, Jawahar Singh left.

Maulvi Karamat Ali said to the subedar, 'Why don't you send a man to Nawabganj too? So we know how many soldiers have arrived there.'

'I can go to Nawabganj,' volunteered Riyaz.

'Raja Sahib plans to send you somewhere else,' replied the subedar. 'I told him about the arrest of the firangis and their journey to Mankapur, and he was very happy. He doesn't want non-combatants to be hurt or killed, and tomorrow he plans on making us swear an oath over this.'

Laxman Pandey proudly announced, 'Well of course, we are his subjects and we must do his bidding.'

'Yes,' replied the subedar. 'From now on, we are his servants.'

Riyaz remained silent, paying close attention to their conversation. The subedar continued, 'As soon as we get news of the safety of Maulvi Sahib, our battalion will set out for Nawabganj, and we shall march to Lucknow.'

'Yes, but as long as we are here, we should not sit around idly. We should try and get news of the enemy's movements and plans,' advised Riyaz.

'Raja Sahib has sent his riders in all directions,' replied the subedar, 'and they are continuously updating us on the situation.'

'Riyaz will be adept at finding out the plans of the enemies,' suggested Maulvi Karamat Ali. 'And if Raja Sahib gives him this responsibility, he can go to Lucknow and see what the situation is like.'

'I shall ask Raja Sahib tomorrow,' said the subedar, getting up to leave. 'Now, all of you should go and rest.'

Riyaz, too, stood up as the subedar said, 'You can go home now, Riyaz.'

'Very good.'

He offered a salaam to the subedar and, chatting with Laxman Pandey and Jawahar Singh, reached the field where the soldiers were cooking their dinner.

'Riyaz Bhaiyya, go home now,' said Laxman Pandey.

Riyaz took Maulvi Sahib aside, said something to him, left the orchard and went to his house via the dust track. Riyaz's father, having already heard that the army had arrived, had just come out of his house. Riyaz said salaam from a distance and, coming closer, bent down to hug him. They entered the house together. Riyaz's mother heard his voice and excitedly came towards the *deohri* and embraced him. Blessing him, she asked, 'Son, you came two hours ago but are only reaching home now?'

'Amma, there were some army matters. Subedar Sahib had gone for an audience with Raja Sahib, and it was only when he returned that I got permission to come home.'

His younger brother and sister also came out. He ate dinner with his father and brother, after which they sat on charpoys in the courtyard to catch up.

Rustam Ali Khan said, 'Sayyid Wajid Hussain came from Lucknow today and said that the English have started surrounding Qilas and white soldiers have been called to be stationed at the Residency.'

'But how long can 1000 or 1200 firangis fight us?' said Riyaz. 'One day, they will have to lay down their weapons.'

'They have a huge cantonment in Kanpur,' replied Rustam Ali Khan, 'I'm sure they will get help from there.'

'Abba Mian, they won't even get a chance to leave Kanpur.'

'These firangis are very cunning,' replied Riyaz's father. 'They never openly confront anyone. They fight using deception and duplicity.'

'You are right. Subedar Sahib was also saying this. But now, their cunning will come to nothing. All our forces have gathered in Nawabganj,* and as soon as Raja Sahib orders, we too shall march there and head towards Lucknow.'

'But I don't understand one thing, Riyaz Mian. How can an army fight without a commander? Every regiment and every battalion will be an independent unit.'

'Yes,' replied Riyaz, 'but any day now, Maulvi Ahmadullah Shah will be freed from the firangis' prison, and the armies will fight under his command.'

---

* By 23 June, Nawabganj had become a centre for the mutineers.

'And if for some reason he is not freed, then what?' asked Rustam Ali Khan.

'Today is the ninth of June,★ and Faizabad is under our control. Actually, the army is doing everything under the directions of Maulvi Ahmadullah Shah. He is issuing orders from jail.'

'God willing that this should happen,' sighed Riyaz's father. 'Our Raja Sahib is also waiting for him to be freed. He has already put together 5000 infantry and cavalrymen to take part in the War of Independence and has ordered an army of the Pasis to be deployed. Thakur Loni Singh of Mithauli is also making similar preparations.'

'What is your plan?' Riyaz asked his father.

'Raja Sahib will hand me the command of the cavalry. He told me to be ready.'

'How many cavalrymen are there in Mahmudabad right now?'

'Six hundred in total,' replied Rustam Ali Khan. 'Three hundred from Mahmudabad and another 300 from the surrounding areas. All are well trained and carry weapons.'

'Will Raja Sahib also go?'

'Yes, he will lead his own forces. The firangis sent a messenger, asking Raja Sahib to affirm loyalty to them by sending money and soldiers. Raja Sahib sent the messenger back, saying that there were neither soldiers nor any money in Mahmudabad.'

★ On 9 June, the flag of revolt against the angrez was raised in Faizabad. Maulvi Ahmadullah Shah was freed from jail and, after being given a gun salute, was made commander of the rebels.

Riyaz said, 'But the angrez have new cannons and we don't.'

'Hindustani artillery has similar cannons but smaller. They'll do the job,' explained Rustam Ali Khan. 'More than having superior artillery, it is important to have one's wits about in the battlefield. A soldier should never be afraid.'

'Abba Mian, I am not afraid,' Riyaz earnestly declared. 'I just told you about the whole affair of the firangis, whom my companions wanted to kill. But I stood in front of them like a shield and saved them.'

'Son, God in all his mercy will bless you for this,' Rustam Ali Khan said. 'Whoever behaves in a just manner with enemies and shows them mercy is truly a brave man. You have done well. Raja Sahib also believes in this. He sent some fifteen or twenty firangi women and children, under the protection of his soldiers, to Lucknow.'

'Yes, I heard,' replied Riyaz. 'I also heard that the firangis did not even thank their escort when they arrived in Lucknow.'

'It's not quite like that,' interjected Rustam Ali Khan. 'The women praised the soldiers in front of the commissioner. It was the behaviour of the officers that was not proper.'

Riyaz's mother interrupted the conversation. 'You can continue tomorrow morning. Let him sleep now. Who knows when he last slept on a bed.'

'Fine. You rest now, son.' Rustam Ali Khan said.

Riyaz was absolutely exhausted. As soon as he lay down, he fell asleep. When Riyaz awoke, Rustam Ali Khan had already left for the mosque for the dawn prayers. Riyaz carried out his ablutions, went to the mosque and prayed in congregation. On his return, at the entrance of a nearby house, he saw Shiv Pratap Singh, head of Raja Sahib's security detail, talking to someone.

As soon as Shiv Pratap Singh saw the father-and-son duo, he offered his salaam, asked after the family and their health, and said, 'Riyaz Mian, I have come looking for you. Raja Sahib has asked to see you. I went looking for you at the place where your men are camped.'

'Thakur Sahib, I came home at night.'

Shiv Pratap Singh now addressed Riyaz's father, 'Risaldar Sahib, Raja Sahib has asked to see you too.' Chatting with each other, they proceeded towards the Qila. After speaking to Raja Sahib for nearly two hours, Riyaz and his father returned home.

'Where did you go from the mosque?' asked Riyaz's mother as they entered the house. 'Breakfast is getting cold.'

'Raja Sahib had asked to see us. We ate breakfast there.'

As Riyaz started wearing his uniform, his mother asked, 'Do you have to return to your platoon right now?'

'I am just going for a short while now but will leave in the afternoon.'

'For where?'

'I'm going to Lucknow.'

He left for the orchard. His companions were sitting around and chatting under the shade of the trees, and Subedar Sahib, with his hands on his hips, was pacing to and fro in front of his tent. Riyaz walked up to the subedar, and they saluted each other.

'I just received orders from Raja Sahib. You should leave for Lucknow by afternoon and take Laxman Pandey, Ramzan Khan and Jawahar Singh with you. Jawahar can then leave for Faizabad.'

'Very good,' replied Riyaz. 'But none of them have horses.'

'Horses will be arranged. You go home and rest. Be back here by noon.'

Taking his leave, Riyaz went to chat briefly with his friends and then headed home. His mother said, 'Son, why don't you rest? I shall wake you up by eleven o'clock. By then, lunch will also be ready.'

He took off his uniform and stretched out on the bed. At eleven, his sister woke him up. He took a quick bath and went to the courtyard, to talk to his father. At 11.30 a.m., he ate his lunch and, exactly at noon, returned to the camp.

The subedar called him into his tent and, handing him an envelope, said, 'Hide this in such a way that even if you are searched no one is able to find it. As soon as you reach Lucknow, give this to Raja Jai Lal Singh, who will meet you at Shah Ji Ki Deohri. Repeat whatever Raja Sahib has told you to him.'

He took the envelope and was just about to leave when the subedar said, 'Oh, I forgot to tell you. Take off your uniform and wear civilian clothes. I have also told your companions.'

Riyaz offered his salaams as he left the tent.

4

Arrest

Riyaz, Laxman, Ramzan Khan and Jawahar Singh rode like the wind, and by 8 p.m. they had covered more than half the distance. They reached a village to rest for the night. The village chief invited them to sleep in his quarters. As soon as day broke, they left for Lucknow.

They bumped into some cavalrymen near a village called Madkipur. Riyaz recognized one of them—his name was Khudadaad Khan, a native of Bulundshahr. Until two months ago he had been in Sitapur, so Riyaz asked him how things were in that town.

Khudadaad Khan looked around and whispered to Riyaz, 'Khan Sahib, it is not a good idea to speak here. Let's go into the thicket over there.'

So Khudadaad Khan, Riyaz and their comrades went down into the thicket, tied their horses to some bushes and sat on the ground. Khudadaad Khan said to Riyaz, 'Time is flying by, and there's no knowing what will happen when.'

'Why are the armies still quiet?' Laxman asked.

'The governor general has made Sir Henry Lawrence★ brigadier general. He is very cruel. He has hanged dozens of innocent people until now. There is no question of a fair hearing. He doesn't listen to anyone. He calls people from the royal family and abuses them.'

'And they remain quiet?' asked Ramzan Khan.

'What can they do except stay quiet?' countered a comrade of Khudadaad Khan's. Just four or six days ago, he sent four notables to the gallows for the crime of not offering their salaams to him.'

Riyaz paused to think, then asked, 'What other news?'

'The troops have been moved from the Daulat Khana† to Machchi Bhawan. The magazine has also been moved there, and the whiteys from the 32nd have been sent to Mandiaown and Madkipur, so that we cannot do anything against them.'

★ On 3 May, the 7th Awadh Irregular Infantry rose up in mutiny. Sir Henry Lawrence immediately quashed their rebellion. The situation was becoming worse, so the governor general gave Sir Henry Lawrence the powers of a brigadier general. The commander of the armies in Awadh was Brigadier Henderson, who was a subordinate of the Kanpur Division's commanding officer, Major General Sir Hugh Massy Wheeler. But because of the changing circumstances, the governor general had made him a deputy to the chief commissioner of Awadh, Sir Henry Lawrence.

† Daulat Khana was the old residence of Nawab Asaf-ud-Daula. One part of it is nowadays called Sheesh Mahal. There were a number of buildings in the Daulat Khana. When Asaf-ud-Daula and his court moved from Faizabad to Lucknow, they put up in these buildings. The most famous building among these was called Asafi Kothi. After the demise of Asaf-ud-Daula, Sadat Ali Khan moved to Farhat Bakhsh.

'Bhai, I am surprised that all this is happening, and our armies are just sitting twiddling their thumbs. If the firangs get help from Bengal or the Punjab, we shan't be able to do anything.'

In a secretive tone, Khudadaad Khan said, 'Maulvi Sahib was freed from prison yesterday. I just got the information this morning. Whatever he orders shall be done.'

Laxman Pandey asked, 'Are those coming from outside being questioned?'

'Of course, they are,' retorted Umrao Baig, a friend of Khudadaad Khan's. *Kashtiyon ka pul*★ has been brought near the Residency, and there is a checkpoint there, manned continuously by the whiteys. Whoever they suspect, they take into custody. Earlier they used to lock them up in the basement of Machchi Bhawan, but now they just hang them.'

Khudadaad Khan interrupted, 'You shouldn't go this way. Go towards Nishatganj, and you will find boats to take you across.'

Riyaz consulted his comrades. Jawahar Singh said, 'Instead of crossing the bridge, we should go by boat.'

'Do you have any news regarding the whereabouts of Raja Jai Lal Singh?' Riyaz asked Khudadaad Khan.

'He is in Lucknow. I just saw him with Rukn-ud-Daula, you will find him at Shah Ji Ki Deohri.'

★ *Kashtiyon ka pul*, or a bridge of boats, was initially made near Moti Mahal, but before the War of Independence started, Sir Henry Lawrence ordered the bridge to be brought closer to the Residency. It was placed opposite the Residency's cannons.

'Right, we'll be off then,' Riyaz said as he looked around. 'When do you plan to come?'

Khudadaad Khan replied, 'Very soon.'

'In two to four days, we shall all be here. My platoon will leave for Nawabganj today, and I too plan on going from here to Nawabganj tomorrow.'

'Khan Sahib, be very careful when you enter the city,' Khudadaad Khan cautioned. 'The firangis have let loose their spies, who are everywhere, always passing on information.'

Jawahar Singh asked Khudadaad Khan, 'Listen, Khan Sahib. Three or four days ago, did four men and three women from Sitapur pass through here?'

'Yes, they did. Four men and three women, of whom one was a young woman. A zamindar's workers brought them in a closed bullock cart.'

'It was we who sent them!' Riyaz exclaimed.

'You made a mistake,' replied Khudadaad Khan. 'Those bastards should have been killed here. They have been so cruel.'

'We mustn't forget the ways of our ancestors,' rebutted Riyaz. 'If the English are being cruel, God will punish them.'

Riyaz and his companions emerged from the thicket and went towards a narrow, dusty road. They mounted their horses and rode for Nishatganj.

Ramzan Khan said, 'We should enter the city separately and meet at Shah Ji Ki Deohri.'

'That's a good idea,' Riyaz said.

Talking among themselves, they reached Nishatganj. After eating breakfast at a halwai's shop, they crossed the

river by boat. Near Shah Najaf, there were some fifteen
or twenty soldiers looking towards Moti Mahal. Riyaz and
his comrades were in the shadows, on the riverbank. One
by one, Riyaz sent his comrades ahead and, after half an
hour, set off himself. Travelling via Sultanganj, he reached
Chowpad Kay Astabal. It was empty, and so he set off
towards Darush-Shifa. On the way, he spotted two soldiers
from the 48th. He stopped them and asked for Risaldar
Barkat Ahmad's address. One of them replied, 'He has
either gone somewhere or gone underground.'

'Do you know anything about Captain Alamgir Khan?'

'Yes, he should be at the Residency right now.'

He said goodbye to them and entered the city via
Maindu Khan Ki Chaoni. The streets were empty. If
someone appeared, he would, on seeing Riyaz, disappear
into the alleyways. Riyaz reached Rakabganj, where some
shops were open and a few people were going about their
business. He stopped his horse near a cloth merchant's shop
and dismounted. The shopkeeper offered his salaams in a
fearful voice. Riyaz greeted him in return and asked, 'Is the
bazaar closed today?'

'Yes, sir. For days now, this is how it has been,' replied
the shopkeeper and paused for a moment. 'Perhaps you are
from out of town?'

'Yes, I am a *pardesi*.'

'You should go wherever you plan to, because if the
firangis or the kotwali get wind of you, they will lock you
up immediately. There is a new firangi officer, and he has
created hell. If this continues for another few days, the army
will revolt, and the city will also join them to seek revenge.'

'Don't worry, everything will work out very soon,' Riyaz tried to assure him. 'If you know anything about Syed Barkat Ahmad, please tell me. Where I can find him?'

The shopkeeper looked at him suspiciously and said, 'Sahib, us shopkeepers, we just sit at our shops from morning to evening. What could we possibly tell you?'

Realizing that he would get no more information here, Riyaz quickly mounted his horse and went to Shah Ji Ki Deohri via Gol Darwaza. Jawahar Singh had already reached, but Ramzan Khan and Laxman Pandey had still not arrived.

As soon as Jawahar Singh saw him, he said, 'Raja Jai Lal Singh is in that haveli facing us. Near the Deohri is a tonga which will take you to him.'

'And you?' asked Riyaz, 'Will you just stay here?'

'Yes, I shall wait for Laxman Pandey and Ramzan Khan.'

'Fine. I'll be back soon.'

Riyaz spurred his horse towards the haveli. An armed guard was standing inside the deohri. Riyaz tied his horse to a peg on the ground and approached the soldier.

The soldier immediately levelled his rifle at him and, in a menacing tone, asked, 'Who are you?'

'A friend, a neighbour from the north.'

'A neighbour from the north' was the secret code that Raja Sahib had told him about. The soldier lowered his rifle and asked in a friendly voice, 'Couldn't you have come in the darkness of the night, under the cover of the stars?'

'I left after the break of dawn.'

'Have you come alone?'

'No. I have three companions. Tell Raja Sahib that I have come from Mahmudabad.'

The soldier called out to someone, 'Bholay Bhaiyya, tell the groom that the molasses are here.'

Riyaz understood that they were being secretive and went closer to the soldier. 'Is there a fear of spies even here?'

'More than elsewhere,' the soldier replied. 'Even I might be a spy. The firangis have opened up their wallets. Now, a daughter tells on her father and a father spies on his son.'

Riyaz stood behind the door. After a few minutes, the man returned and motioned to the soldier. The soldier directed Riyaz to the man, and Riyaz followed him in.

Raja Jai Lal Singh was sitting in a well-appointed room, smoking a hookah. Riyaz leaned forward to offer his salaam and then quietly presented him with the envelope. Jai Lal Singh opened the envelope, took out the letter and asked Riyaz to sit near him.

'Khan Sahib, I know your father well, but until now I haven't had the pleasure of meeting you. Tell me, how are things in your area?'

Riyaz recounted some of his experiences in the army. 'From here I will go to Nawabganj, and from there we will march on to Lucknow after three or four days. Please keep the city folk ready, for we will come knocking down the telegraph wires.'

'The city folk are ready and waiting for an indication,' said Jai Lal Singh. 'Lawrence has created armed divisions and is preparing to fight under siege, but we are not worried about his defences.'

Riyaz asked, 'What arrangements have been made for cannonballs and gunpowder?'

'Magazines have been stashed in various parts of the city and, as we speak, guns, ammunition and gunpowder are being gathered.'

'Raja Sahib has said that we must capture the firangis' magazines, as they have tonnes of gunpowder.'

'Yes, there was a magazine in the Daulat Khana, but it has been moved to Machchi Bhawan, and that is what we will capture first.'

'This is why I have come to you, because if the firangis save their magazines or destroy them, it will be more difficult for us.'

'Tell Raja Sahib not to worry. I have already sent some men disguised as labourers to Machchi Bhawan and have given them complete instructions.'

A servant interrupted their conversation, 'Sarkar, another three guests have arrived.'

Riyaz immediately replied, 'Yes, they are my comrades.'

'Take the horses to the stables and prepare a room upstairs for the guests,' instructed Jai Lal Singh.

Riyaz said, 'Please take my horse, too. It is near the deohri—a dappled horse.'

The servant bowed, offered his salaams and left. Jawahar Singh, Laxman Pandey and Ramzan Khan arrived. Jai Lal Singh greeted them and said, 'Khan Sahib, why don't you all stay here? Wash and rest. Tomorrow, I will give you a letter for your subedar.'

'As you wish,' replied Riyaz. 'But I would also like to meet Risaldar Syed Barkat Ahmad by this evening if possible.'

'I shall send a man to make an appointment with him for late afternoon. You can return before sunset.'

'Yes, I will try and return even earlier.'

Riyaz and his comrades retired to their quarters, bathed and rested until noon. They had lunch and, in the late afternoon, Riyaz went to see Syed Barkat Ahmad, accompanied by Raja Jai Lal Singh's attendant. Syed Barkat Ahmad was staying in a building near the Residency, but apart from his close comrades, no one knew anything about his whereabouts. He was an old friend of Riyaz's father—both had been posted in the royal cantonment together. He embraced Riyaz warmly and asked after his father.

Riyaz debriefed him about his family and the recent events, adding, 'I am surprised that you are still quiet.'

'We are waiting for Maulvi Sahib. He was freed from prison yesterday, and in a day or two he will leave Faizabad. As soon as he arrives in Lucknow, we will surround the firangis.'

'Yes, we shouldn't delay any further. Abba wants you to first and foremost capture the magazine.'

'We have made the preparations. Raja Jai Lal Singh has sent Azeemullah Khan, and ten others are there already.'

'What is your opinion about the city dwellers?'

'You must have heard of Mir Muhtasham Bilgrami. Well, he has really set back the whiteys and the Company's soldiers near Gonda and Bahraich.'

'Yes, of course. Who isn't familiar with him? I have met him twice. I also know Mustapha Khan and Mirza Haider Baig, who have been fighting for ages.'

Syed Barkat Ahmad replied, 'They are the original fighters of this War of Independence, which started fifteen years ago. They have the opportunity to not only obtain independence but also show their own talent.'

Riyaz said, 'If there is time tomorrow morning, I shall definitely try to meet them.'

'They congregate at Mustapha Khan's house in the evenings,' Syed Barkat Ahmad said. 'Mustapha Khan lives near Bagh-e-Qazi, and if you can, you should go and meet them tonight. Mir Muhtasham Bilgrami may leave for Malihabad tomorrow.'

'I shall try and meet them tonight, get the lay of the land and an idea of what the city folk are thinking.'

'On his word, 10,000 armed men will take to the streets.'

Riyaz left the cavalryman Syed Barkat Ahmad's house at five in the evening. Dressed like a Lucknow-wallah, Riyaz was carrying a light sword and two pistols were tucked in his cummerbund. An aunt of his lived in Yahya Ganj, and he went to see her. After sunset, he went to see Mustapha Khan with her son, Mannan Khan.

Mustapha Khan's door was closed, but a man on the street, who was carrying a *lota*, recognized Mannan Khan.

'Khan Sahib, there is a meeting in Pakariya Waali Kothi.'

Mannan Khan entered another alley. Riyaz asked him, 'Is there no building with that name in Lucknow?'

Mannan smiled. 'Oh, it's a make-believe name.'

'So where are we going now?'

'Muhtasham Sahib's house. Everyone will be there,' replied Mannan Khan.

Chatting away, they went towards Mir Muhtasham's house. They were both called inside. Mirza Haider Baig, Thakur Matwala and Mir Muhtasham were on the second floor of the house, talking among each other. Riyaz had already met Mir Muhtasham. After offering salaams and a bit of chit-chat, he went into one of the rooms with him. Muhtasham was in a hurry. So they spoke quickly and Riyaz left for Gol Darwaza.

The bazaar had already been shut, and people were rushing home. Lucknow's famous bustling streets and buzzing atmosphere had vanished; there was terror in the air. He reached Daryaee Tola via Raja Ki Bazaar and had just set off for Chah Kankar when four *barqandaaz** emerged from an alley, blocked his way and demanded, 'Where are you going?'

'M'ali Khan Ki Serai,' Riyaz replied without hesitation.

'Are you staying in the Serai?' asked one of the soldiers.

'No, I am not. Why, what's the matter?'

'You are not from the city. You'll have to come with us to the kotwali.'

'But why?' asked Riyaz.

A soldier shoved his rifle into Riyaz's chest and ordered, 'Don't you move.'

The other soldier disarmed Riyaz with lightning speed, taking away his pistols.

'What do you people want?' Riyaz asked the watchmen.

'Kotwal Sahib will answer you,' said the soldier who'd taken away Riyaz's arms. 'We were ordered to arrest you.'

---

* Night watchmen.

The soldiers also took away his sword and brought him before the kotwal. Mirza Reza Ali Baig looked Riyaz up and down and asked, 'What is your good name?'

'I am called Riyaz Ahmad Khan.'

'Khan Sahib, the deputy commissioner has ordered your arrest and asked for you to be taken to the Residency immediately.'

Riyaz lowered his head to think. Reza Ali Baig paused for a second and resumed, 'Deputy Commissioner Bahadur is there right now, waiting for you.'

Riyaz understood from the kotwal's manner that he had been recognized. The kotwal asked for his carriage. He got in, sat beside Riyaz and said to one of the watchmen, 'Twelve mounted soldiers will accompany me.'

'Very well, Your Excellency,' replied a hawaldar as he bowed down to offer his salaam. 'Enayat Baig!' the kotwal got angry. 'Aren't you familiar with police regulations? If any officer saw you offering salaam like this, you would be fired on the spot.'

On the way, the kotwal asked Riyaz, 'Khan Sahib, whom did you come here to meet?'

'I have dozens of relations in the city,' Riyaz replied dryly.

'You met cavalryman Barkat Ahmad, didn't you?'

'Kotwal Sahib, you will not get anywhere with this. You want to present me to the deputy commissioner? Take me there. I don't want to talk anymore.'

Ali Reza Baig stared at Riyaz, thinking of something.

5

Set Free

The room in which Riyaz was imprisoned had just one skylight. After a while, he started feeling very hot and lay down on the floor. He thought of his old parents. After an hour or so, he heard the sound of a door opening but kept lying where he was. Someone with a heavy step came inside. Riyaz crooked his neck to see who it was and, recognizing him, immediately stood up.

The man was one of the people he had saved from his comrades near the Sarayan. The old man smiled and came forward to shake his hand. Riyaz, too, greeted him with a smile and said, 'You recognized me?'

'Yes, I was just informed,' said the old man. 'And I cannot forget my saviour. We do not forget those who help us.'

Riyaz replied, 'And in return for that help, I have been locked up in this dark, airless room.'

'Mr Riyaz, the Indian armies are mutinying, and you too are a junior officer in one of these armies.'

'Yes, but I never caused you any bodily discomfort or pain.'

'This is why I have come, so that I can take you outside,' the old firangi said. 'I have just told the chief commissioner what a brave and merciful young man you are. You are different from those rebels who are slaughtering Englishmen.'

'I am against killing and terror,' replied Riyaz. 'But I am not complaining to you that you have locked me up in this small room in the heat.'

'Come. Come outside with me. My name is Joseph Filton.'

Riyaz left the little room with him. He was drenched in sweat. Mr Filton took him towards the gardens and motioned at a two-storey building. 'I am staying in Maisher Mall, Mr Gomes's house. Come and meet Sir Henry Lawrence. I am sure you will be happy to meet him, and you will know that we are not what the Indians think we are.'

Mr Filton entered the Residency gates. There were armed guards everywhere. Mr Filton took Riyaz to the chief commissioner's room. Riyaz saluted the officer as they do in the army and stood before him.

Sir Henry Lawrence was sitting in a chair and staring at Riyaz, as if he was trying to read his thoughts from his facial expressions. Riyaz didn't like the sunken cheeks and the whitish complexion. Sir Henry stared at him for two minutes and then, in a superior voice, said, 'Please sit down, Mr Riyaz. I appreciate your services, but due to the circumstances I have no choice but to have you arrested.'

Riyaz sat down on a chair near Sir Henry's desk. Mr Filton also found a chair and started speaking to Sir Henry in English. Riyaz had developed a rudimentary understanding of English since joining the army. Mr Filton was praising Riyaz, on whom Sir Henry had his eyes fixed. As soon as Mr Filton fell silent, Sir Henry said to Riyaz, 'You seem like a civilized young man. By saving my fellow Englishmen and women, you have done my people a favour. You are a good fellow. Living among the mutineers, you are merely supporting them on principle.'

'I am grateful that you have acknowledged my deeds. But I have done no favour to you or to your people by saving those Englishmen and women. I have merely done my duty. The humanitarian code dictates that we are all bound to each other through basic rights and duties.'

'You seem like a well-educated man, Mr Riyaz,' said Sir Henry. 'If you leave the mutineers, I see a very good future for you.'

'We have a difference of opinion,' Riyaz solemnly replied. 'I can see what you are implying, but I have nothing to say about it.'

'Listen, this mutiny is just a little blip. It will last for a few days at the most. The Indians are breaking the peace and spreading discord. Neither are they united, nor do they have any one leader. All they want to do is kill and loot, and that is exactly what they're doing. We are fighting for a purpose, and however much you disagree with that purpose, you cannot refute the fact that if the mutineers are allowed to do whatever they wish, entire cities will be uprooted and human life will have no worth.'

'I am here in front of you as a prisoner,' Riyaz replied emphatically, 'which is why this conversation serves no purpose. Even if we assume the impossible—that we will change each other's views—this will not make any difference to the rest of the armies, as I am not their representative.'

'Well, why don't you just decide for yourself then? You seem like a promising young man, and if you help us, we will reward you in good measure. We will make you someone.'

Riyaz bowed his head, pausing to think about what to say. 'In the current circumstances, I cannot help you in any way.'

'Try to understand my position,' Sir Henry said tersely. 'You are a mutineer and will be hanged, but I am giving you a chance to think about my offer. You will be put up in an airy and well-lit room while you do this.'

He stood up, as did Riyaz and Mr Filton. Sir Henry called in a young Englishman, said something quietly to him and left. Mr Filton wanted to talk to Riyaz, but the young Englishman didn't give him a chance. He took Riyaz to a double-storey house within the Residency and locked him up. The room had two skylights, which let in fresh air and natural light. The door was made of iron rods instead of having a *chilman*. There was a bed and a chair in the room.

Riyaz sat on the chair; his thoughts drifted towards home and his elderly parents. He thought of what they would go through when they found out about his arrest.

Mr Filton came to see him again in the afternoon, accompanied by another Englishman and a lady. The lady's name was Mrs Prill Forbes. They tried to reason with him for a long time. After they left, an Indian soldier brought Riyaz some food. Riyaz ate and fell asleep. In the afternoon, some Englishmen came to look at him, took a peek at him from outside the room and left. In the evening, Sir Henry Lawrence called for Riyaz. He told him about the events in Kanpur and said, 'I assure you that your loyalty will be well rewarded. Just tell me what Raja Loni Singh* of Mithauli and Raja Nawab Ali of Mahmudabad are planning.'

'You are trying to test my loyalty, but a man can only be loyal to one person or one idea.'

'Listen, young man! I am giving you one more opportunity to think this over. Sleep over it tonight. You saved some Englishmen's lives, and so I do not want to punish you in the manner which mutineers deserve.'

Riyaz kept silent. Sir Henry Lawrence motioned to two sentries, each of whom held one of Riyaz's arms and escorted him back to the room.

Riyaz offered his evening prayers and started pacing to and fro within the confines of the room. After an hour, an Englishman took him to an Indian officer. The Englishman said to the officer, 'Risaldar Sahib, this is our guest. Please eat with him and bring him back to me.'

The risaldar wanted to ask something, but the Englishman left with another officer. He took Riyaz to the room that served as the mess for Indian officers. A few officers were sitting around, and as soon as Riyaz entered,

---

* Raja Loni Singh was a big taluqdar from the Khairabad district. He governed over a large area and had a big fort in Mithauli. Like other taluqdars, he too took part in the battle for independence in 1857. He sent armies of Pasis and Beragiyons to Lucknow and fought till the end.

they all turned to stare at him. The risaldar sat down, pushed a chair towards Riyaz and said to him, 'My young friend, I just heard that fate has blessed you and that the chief commissioner bahadur has promised to give you a land grant.'

'Yes,' Riyaz replied, 'I have been told this many times since morning.'

'You should take advantage of this opportunity. It is the only intelligent thing to do. Such opportunities do not come again.'

'My dear sir, you are of course right. But I am not an opportunist.'

'I don't think you have understood what I am saying,' said the risaldar in a friendly tone.

'No, I understand what you are getting at. I want an ashrafi and I am being offered a paisa. You tell me, how can I accept this offer?'★

The risaldar did not understand and looked confusedly at Riyaz.

Riyaz explained, 'I want the entire country and I am being offered a piddling bit of land. Now you tell me, how can I accept this land grant?'

'My young friend, I do not think that you properly appreciate our circumstances. If you think that the English are going to leave India, that is absolutely impossible.'

'Risaldar Sahib, I am sorry but it is you who has no idea of the ground reality. Hundreds of thousands of troops are already battle-ready.'

★ Translator's note: An ashrafi is a gold coin, and a paisa refers to a copper coin.

'That won't make a difference. The English have new weapons, they are more disciplined and organized, and their armies are well trained.'

'They do not have our passion. We fight for our homeland, while they fight only for their stomachs,' exclaimed Riyaz.

The risaldar was taken aback.

'Risaldar Sahib, I am telling you the truth. You will see in a few days what will happen to this system.'

A man walked in and took the risaldar to another room.

'Listen, this young man is from a well-respected family from Mahmudabad, and I have just found out that the chief commissioner bahadur is going to give him a high rank in the army. So please don't do anything that will make him more averse to us.'

'Captain Hare has told me everything,' replied the risaldar. He sat next to Riyaz. They ate, and half an hour later, two Englishmen appeared and escorted Riyaz to the room again.

There was a candle flickering in the room. The Englishmen locked the door from the outside. Riyaz offered his night prayers, put out the candle with his fingers and stretched out on the bed. There was a breeze coming in, and he quickly fell asleep. But then, on hearing the door open, he woke up with a jolt.

Riyaz sat up and stared at the door. In the darkness, he watched a shadow drifting into the room. Someone dressed in black was coming towards the bed, ensuring that their steps made no noise.

'Who are you?' Riyaz demanded.

'Mr Riyaz?' someone said in a feminine voice.

The voice was of an English lady. Riyaz stood up in surprise.

'Mr Riyaz, it's me,' she whispered.

Riyaz had recognized the voice—of the girl he had saved near the Sarayan.

'It's me, Alice.' She came closer still. 'Alice Harrison. Do you recognize me?'

'Yes,' replied Riyaz, bewildered. 'But why are you here so late at night?'

'I have come to save your life,' Ms Alice Harrison said quietly. 'You . . . you saved mine. Today, I have got an opportunity to help you.'

Riyaz was baffled and didn't know what to say. Alice put her hand on his shoulder and said, 'Please sit down. No one will come here until four in the morning.'

Riyaz sat on the bed. Alice sat next to him and whispered, 'Tomorrow, the chief commissioner will call for you one last time, and if you don't accept his offer, he will send you to Machchi Bhawan, where you will be hanged.'

'I am ready for that.'

'Mr Riyaz, are you not afraid of death?'

'I am a Muslim. I am only afraid of God.'

'Sir Henry Lawrence is ready to offer you a big landholding.'

'Ah, so this is his last move,' said Riyaz with a smile. '*He* has sent you.'

'No! Not at all. Believe me, I have come on my own and no one has sent me. I came here on my own.'

'Why?'

'To free you from prison.'

Riyaz paused and said, 'Well, if you can free me from here somehow, I will be forever grateful.'

'Really, this is why I've come.'

'Will you be questioned?'

'No one knows that I am here. Even if they do find out, the most that can happen is that I will be shot for treason.'

'If this is how it is, then you cannot endanger your life on my account.'

'It might not be this way. But if it is, I shall happily hand myself over to the authorities.'

'But why are you doing this?'

'You saved my life. I shall save yours.' Alice stared at him through the darkness and said, 'You are a chivalrous young man. You have chosen to fight for the freedom of your homeland.' Her voice became louder and more passionate. 'Mr Riyaz, you really are an exceptional man, a role model for others. The kind of man whose deeds people sing songs about.'

'You are getting carried away by your emotions, Ms Alice. Your voice is becoming louder. If anyone sees you, what will they say?'

'Oh! Mr Riyaz, how sweet you are!' Alice replied, lowering her voice. 'Even in these circumstances, you are worried about my honour. Mothers who have sons like you are truly blessed.'

She fell silent and turned to look towards the door. Riyaz also looked that way. He listened closely and realized someone was pacing down the veranda.

'Someone is coming this way,' whispered Alice.

'It's a soldier. I can tell from the sound of the shoes. There are nails fixed into the soles.'

Alice hid in the corner by the door. A few seconds later, an Englishman came up to the door, peered in and went away. As the footsteps receded, Alice sat next to Riyaz again and said, 'I thought no one would be here before four o'clock. It looks like the guard has been doubled.'

'So it should be. I am a very dangerous mutineer!'

'Don't worry. I shall take you safely outside the Residency walls right now!'

'Ms Alice, I implore you. Leave me to my fate.'

'I am going to go and get an Indian soldier's uniform. You put it on and leave this place.'

Without waiting for an answer, she left the room and returned with a small bundle. As she gave it to Riyaz, she said, 'There is a pistol in this, and outside you will find a rifle too.'

'Ms Alice, how can I ever thank you enough?' Riyaz said as he stared at her luminous face.

'There is no need to thank me, but promise that you will never forget me.'

'Ms Alice!' Riyaz exclaimed, overcome with emotion.

'M M M . . . Mr Riyaz,' stuttered Alice as the words got lost in the darkness. She put her hands on his shoulders.

Riyaz felt as if a lightning bolt had hit him. His body trembled, but he immediately regained hold of his senses, picked up the bundle and went into the adjoining room.

6

The Confabulations

On 18 June 1857, just before noon, Riyaz reached Nawabganj. The Indian Infantry's 22nd division★ had just reached Faizabad and camped in an open space outside the city. The company's commander, Jamadar Harbans Singh, had been posted in Khiri with Riyaz. He welcomed Riyaz and asked him about the situation.

'I'm on my way from Lucknow,' replied Riyaz, 'and my platoon has already left Mahmudabad. They should have arrived here today. I'm surprised they haven't reached yet.'

'Your platoon will come here after nightfall. Why don't you stay in my tent until then?'

Jamadar Harbans Singh's tent had already been erected. He took Riyaz in and asked about the situation in Lucknow.

★ The 22nd Native Infantry Corps, the 6th Awadh Infantry and a light field battery were in Faizabad. On 9 June 1857, these divisions raised the flag of revolt against the English and freed Maulvi Ahmadullah Shah from prison.

Riyaz told him about Risaldar Syed Barkat Ahmad, Raja Jai Lal Singh and Mir Muhtasham. 'I was arrested in Lucknow. A few days earlier, I had saved some English men and women from the men in my troop. One of them was Ms Alice. Somehow, she helped me to escape the prison at night. So I came here.'

'She must be a brave girl! Otherwise most firangis are after our blood,' replied Harbans Singh.

'Yes, if she hadn't set me free, Lawrence would have had me hanged in Machchi Bhawan by now. He has hanged dozens of soldiers already.'

'His days are numbered,' said Harbans Singh. 'Maulvi Sahib has reached Daryabad. He will be here by tomorrow.'

'How many soldiers are with him?' asked Riyaz.

'The 22nd Indian Infantry and 6th Awadh Infantry left Faizabad in front of me, and the divisions from Sultanpur and Raebareli must have joined them. Everyone is coming here.'

'The English are planning to fight under siege,' added Riyaz. 'They have gathered a large quantity of cannons, gunpowder and food. They have also asked for help from Kanpur and Allahabad.'

Jamadar Harbans Singh said, 'By the time help comes we will have made a graveyard for the English in Lucknow. A light artillery division from Shahganj is also coming with Maulvi Sahib.'

'Wasn't there an artillery unit in Faizabad too?' asked Riyaz.

'Yes, it's still there and will leave today.'

Riyaz had been awake all night and, after eating, he went to sleep. He got up at four in the afternoon. By then, a platoon from Bahraich had arrived and set up camp. Their officers were sitting outside Harbans Singh's tent, talking among themselves. Riyaz went and joined them. An officer from the Bahraich Infantry Platoon said, 'I have been told that if we do not get to Lucknow within the next ten days or so, Lawrence will leave with his armies.'

'There are not that many troops in Lucknow,' interjected Riyaz. 'I have just come from there. The English have good long-range cannons and other weapons.'

Another officer said, 'Until they run out of cannons and gunpowder, they will not allow us near the Residency.'

'Yes,' Harbans Singh replied. 'In any case, Maulvi Sahib will be here by tomorrow. Then we will know what to do.'

After a while they all dispersed. By sunset, the 22nd arrived from Mahmudabad. The subedar embraced Riyaz and, patting him on the back, said, 'Riyaz, we had given up on you.'

Riyaz explained everything to him. 'If Alice hadn't saved me, I would have been hanged by now.'

'We heard about your arrest yesterday. If I hadn't seen you today, we would have attacked Lucknow.'

Riyaz undid his *taveez*, took out a folded piece of paper from it and said to the subedar, 'Raja Sahib has written everything in detail.'

The subedar unfolded it and read the letter. He then refolded it and put it away in his pocket, saying, 'A thousand-strong force, loyal to Raja Nawab Ali, will be here by tomorrow. The day after tomorrow, I shall pick 200 cavalrymen and send them to Lucknow. They will enter the city in twos and fours, and will wait until the right time to come out of hiding with their weapons.'

'Will only these many men come from there?' asked Riyaz.

'No, more will come,' replied the subedar. 'Troops loyal to Raja Guru Bakhsh Singh of Ramnagar Dhamedi[*] will also come. They too will reach in a day or two, and there is a small artillery unit with them.'

Riyaz paused to think and said, 'Well, it's a good thing that so many artillery units will be here, but we also need magazines.'

'Magazines are being arranged for. Raja Guru Bakhsh Singh and Raja Nawab Ali[†] are also both preparing another army, which will solely comprise Pasis.'

'I know,' replied Riyaz. 'Raja Jai Lal Singh has also formed a loyal army in Garhi Bilool, and the city folk are ready to fight and die.'

'What have you found out about the soldiers?' asked the subedar.

'They are ready. Syed Barkat Ahmad is happy with their preparation, as is Mir Sahib with his troops. Mustapha Khan

---

[*] Ramnagar Dhamedi was a talluqah near the River Ghaghara. The taluqdar was Raja Guru Bakhsh Singh, a valiant leader in the 1857 war. His troops, along with those of Raja Nawab Ali of Mahmudabad, were instrumental in the siege of Lucknow, and his army continued to fight the British until 1888. It is written in the *Sayyidahpur Gazette* that his troops fought in Badi under the command of Maulvi Ahmadullah Shah, the leader of the War of Independence. The Hindu Raja of Ramnagar Dhamedi and the Muslim Raja of Mahmudabad were blood brothers.

[†] Both Raja Sahib of Ramnagar Dhamedi and Raja Sahib of Mahmudabad prepared a large army of Pasis which was instrumental in the siege of Lucknow.

and Mirza Haider Baig have sent men to Unnao, Parwa, Kanpur, Kannauj, Fatehganj and Farrukhabad to acquire magazines.'

A bugle sounded from the other side of town. The subedar said, 'Perhaps another contingent has arrived from Faizabad.'

Riyaz came out of the camp. Pandey Ji and a few of his comrades were standing on the field, talking to each other. They came up to him when they saw him. Pandey Ji said, 'Someone just arrived from Lucknow and said that Laxman Pandey, Jawahar Singh and Ramzan Khan are all safe and well in Lucknow and will be here tomorrow.'

'Yes, Subedar Sahib just told me.'

Maulvi Barkat Ali emerged from one of the other tents, and they all started conversing. Riyaz was still exhausted and fell asleep after his night prayers, only to be woken up by Maulvi Barkat Ali for the dawn prayers. The soldiers were sleepily putting on their clothes. He went to Subedar Sahib. Outside the subedar's tent, Laxman Pandey, Jawahar Singh and Ramzan Khan were sitting and chatting.

Jawahar Singh hugged Riyaz, while Laxman Pandey and Ramzan Khan shook his hands. Jawahar Singh said, 'Bhaiyya Riyaz, as soon as we heard of your arrest, we started making plans to free you, but they set spies on us too.'

Riyaz told them of his escapades in Lucknow and added, 'Actually, the firangis' spies had been on to us since the morning after we arrived in Lucknow.'

'Yes, Khan Sahib,' replied Laxman Pandey. 'We only realized this after your arrest.'

Ramzan Khan said, 'We were going to leave this morning, but Raja Jai Lal Singh got news of your escape last night, and so we left immediately.'

They could see that the subedar was about to emerge from his tent. The four of them stood up and saluted him in the army style. Jawahar Singh, Laxman Pandey and Ramzan Khan debriefed him, after which Subedar Sahib said, 'A message has just arrived from Mahmudabad. Raja Sahib changed his plans after getting Maulvi Sahib's letter, and he will reach Lucknow by dusk today.'

'Lucknow . . .?' Jawahar Singh said nervously.

'By Lucknow I mean that he is not going to enter the city but will camp somewhere on the outskirts. These changes and this urgency are because of the plans that Maulvi Sahib has drawn up.'

Riyaz interjected, 'Subedar Sahib, I heard in Lucknow that the Indian troops of Awadh will be under the leadership of General Azeemullah Khan?'

'What you've heard is correct,' answered the subedar. 'But I am ready for the battle in Lucknow. Maulvi Sahib will be there.'

'I don't know much about Maulvi Sahib,' said Ramzan Khan. 'All I know is that he is a member of some prominent family from Madras.'

'Yes,' Riyaz said. 'And his title is Dildar Jung.* After the fall of the Muslim rulers of Madras, his family dispersed here

---

* Translator's note: Dildar Jung means Braveheart Warrior. These kinds of titles were often granted in Hyderabad. From this we can deduce that perhaps Maulvi Sahib held a high post in Hyderabad and that his ancestors were from there and later left for Arcot or another Muslim state in south India.

and there. Maulvi Sahib headed north and was educated not only in worldly matters but also in spiritual matters. He is a khalifa of Mihrab Shah Qalandar of Gwalior.'*

'Oh,' exclaimed Ramzan Khan.

'We call him Maulvi Sahib, but he is actually as famous as Shah Sahib. He acquired deep spiritual learning in the company of Hazrat Shah Qalandar, may God be pleased with him. Maulvi Sahib was blessed by him, made a khalifa, and it was with his permission that Maulvi Sahib waged jihad against the British and reached Delhi.'

Laxman Pandey said, 'Bhaiyya, shouldn't the command of the armies be in the hands of a general? I think General Azeemullah Khan would be perfect for this role.'

Subedar Sahib interrupted, 'General Azeemullah Khan has sworn allegiance to Maulvi Sahib. Besides, Maulvi Sahib himself is an experienced general.'

Riyaz said, '10,000 men have already gathered under his flag, and among them are Hindus, Muslims, Christians . . . everyone.'

'Who among the Christians are with them?' asked Ramzan Khan.

'Monsieur Joseph. He used to be a French preacher,' replied Riyaz. 'He once got into *munazerah*† with Maulvi Sahib, who explained the difference between truth and

---

* Mehrab Shah Qalandar's *silsilah*, or spiritual lineage, was from the Chishtiyyah–Qadiriyyah order, and there used to be a crowd of followers with him at all times. His tomb is in Gwalior, just outside the main gate of the fort. Every year, the *urs* or the anniversary of his passing is commemorated by thousands of people.

† Translator's note: *Munazerah* is a theological debate.

falsehood so clearly that ever since he has been an ardent follower of Maulvi Sahib.'

'I trust Maulvi Sahib's leadership,' said the subedar.

Riyaz turned to the subedar and asked, 'But why is our Raja Sahib going there?'

'I just told you. It seems that General Azeemullah Khan will reach there today, and together they will draw up the battle plans.'

'Are you planning on sending a messenger to Raja Sahib today?' asked Riyaz.

'Yes, I'll send someone by afternoon.'

'I'm ready. You can send me,' volunteered Riyaz.

'It's too dangerous for you. The firangis must have sent out patrols looking for you in all directions, and if they even get a whiff of you heading to Lucknow, they will try to nab you.'

'Don't worry about me. They won't be able to even find my footsteps. That was a fluke,' replied Riyaz.

'Fine, then,' said the subedar. 'I shall give you a letter, and you can explain everything else orally.'

Riyaz left after midnight. He reached a small hamlet near Chinhat early in the morning. Raja Jai Lal Singh, Mirza Haider Baig and Mustapha Khan had informers on the outskirts of Lucknow and in surrounding villages, to get fresh information and regular updates. Riyaz already knew about the secret codes and the informers. He didn't have much trouble when he reached there. The village chief put him up at his house. The chief informed him that Raja Nawab Ali would reach Muhibullahpur after sunset. He was planning to arrive with 200 horses and leave before dawn the next day.

Riyaz asked, 'Is anyone else coming?'

'I have heard that General Azeemullah Khan★ is also coming because he wants to consult with the Raja Sahib of Mahmudabad.'

'Have the others heard about this meeting?'

'No, not at all. Raja Sahib's munshi came to me yesterday and said that I am to look after any of his men who pass through and to let them stay if they want to.'

'Yes, I was also told to come to you.'

'Tonight, four cooks and 15–20 servants of Raja Sahib will be staying with me and preparing dinner for the officers.'

'I am glad Raja Sahib made these arrangements,' replied Riyaz. 'It's the right time for them.'

The village chief said, 'The raja is a truly generous man. Recently, between Mahmudabad and Lucknow, in six different towns, he ordered bawarchikhanas to be put up for the Muslims and bhandaras for his Hindu men.'

Riyaz already knew about this—Raja Sahib himself had told him. The chief put a charpoy under the bit of thatched roof outside his hut, where Riyaz fell asleep. At eleven o'clock, the chief woke Riyaz up and said, 'Jamadar Sahib, there are four or five firangis in the orchard!'

★ General Azeemullah Khan was an Afghan but had spent most of his life in India. He was a very handsome and tall man. Wherever he went, heads would turn. He travelled to England, then to France and then, via various other countries, he returned to India. He went to Nawab Wajid Ali Shah's mother and brother in London, and it was there that he was told about the Indian situation. He came back to India, and in Kanpur he met Nana Farnavees and Tana Shah. Soon after, he joined the War of Independence. He swore allegiance to Maulvi Ahmadullah Shah and was a prominent figure in the war of 1857.

'Firangis? Here?' Riyaz woke up like a shot. 'Are they soldiers?'

'They seem like hunters,' replied the chief's son. 'There are also three women with them.'

'Hmm. Well, why don't you watch which way they go.'

The chief left. Riyaz got up, put on his uniform, checked his rifle and slung it across his shoulders, ready to go outside. After ten minutes, the chief returned and said, 'There are eight Indian soldiers with them and also four servants, who are getting ready to prepare dinner. In total there are six firangis and four women. The men seem to be looking for game and are next to Kukrail heading that way.'*

'How do you know?'

'They are taking my son, Matadin, with them.'

'Can I look at them from somewhere?'

'Yes, sir. But you should change out of these clothes and wear kurta pyjama and *mudeytha*.'†

'But I don't have a kurta or the kind of pyjama that Muslims wear.'

'I'll go borrow some from Sheikh Ji.'

The chief left and returned after some time with a kurta, pyjama and some white cloth for the turban. Riyaz changed and, instead of tying a mudeytha, tied a turban like that of a maulvi. The chief went into his house and came out with

---

* Kukrail was a jungle just outside Lucknow, which is now a part of the city.

† Translator's note: Mudeytha is an Awadhi word which is a compound of *moond* (Awadhi for head) and *aitha* (from the root *aithna*, to twist). It is a type of turban that is twisted and then tied on the head in one go.

an *angocha*, which he put on Riyaz's shoulder. He smiled and said, 'Jamadar Sahib, now you really look like a maulvi sahib.'

Riyaz walked to the spot outside the village where 30–35 men were standing underneath a mahua tree next to a well. They were all looking towards the orchard. Some Englishmen, dressed in hunting clothes and with rifles in their hands, were standing in the orchard, speaking to the women. The women also carried rifles. Riyaz recognized them. It was Alice and her mother.

Riyaz's heart beat faster. He stood behind a group of villagers. He had recognized one of the men, too: Henry Macmillan, who had come from Shahjahanpur with Alice. He had saved his life as well. When Macmillan saw Riyaz after he was arrested in Lucknow, he'd urged the chief commissioner to have him shot. Alice had told him this, when she came to set him free. She spoke ill of Macmillan.

After a few minutes, the English left the orchard and, accompanied by four villagers, went towards the wilds. Riyaz returned to the chief's home. He ate some food and had just stretched out on the charpoy to sleep when he saw Matadin, the chief's son.

'What's the matter, son? Why have you returned?'

'One of the memsahibs★ has returned. She fell and hurt her knee.'

'Is she very badly hurt?' asked Riyaz.

'Yes, it must be serious. The firangis tend to be very brave. So it must be serious if she has returned.'

★ Translator's note: Memsahib: Madam as pronounced by the locals.

'Where is she?'

'In the orchard, leaning against a tree.'

'They carry medicines with them . . .'

'She hasn't applied any medicine until now. She seems to be in a lot of pain.'

'Can I see her from near the mahua tree?' asked Riyaz.

'Yes, you can.'

'Let's go. Let me see what's happening from a distance.'

The chief asked with concern, 'Jamadar Sahib, is there any danger?'

'No, there's no danger. Who will recognize me?'

All three left the house. The chief and his son were very nervous. Riyaz tried to reassure them, 'Don't be scared. If you get frightened like this, how will we fight for our freedom? We have to fight these cruel people and throw them out of our country.'

'Yes, Jamadar Sahib, but the fighting hasn't started yet,' the chief replied anxiously. 'I have heard that the firangis have stationed white soldiers in Ismailganj, Mudkipur and Mandiaown, and that their cannons are also at the ready.'

'This is what I need to find out,' Riyaz replied as he navigated through the thatched huts. 'We will fight these people somewhere near here.'

They reached the tree. Matadin motioned towards the orchard and said, 'Look there. She is sitting under the tree.'

Riyaz instantly recognized her. It was Alice. An Indian servant was sitting by her, closing a box, while she wrapped a white bandage around her knee. After staring at her for a few seconds, Riyaz asked Matadin, 'How long before the rest of them return?'

'They won't return before three o'clock. They will eat late.'

'I am going to see her. If she hasn't used any medicine, I shall ask you to come over.' The chief turned white as Riyaz, trying to reassure him, said to Matadin, 'You go and keep watch. If you see the firangis heading back, come and warn me.'

'Bu . . . bu . . . but Jamadar Sahib . . .'

Matadin tried to say something, but Riyaz motioned to him to stay quiet. 'Don't be scared. I am saying something. Just do it.'

'Indian soldiers are there too,' said the chief.

'Don't you worry about that.'

Riyaz went towards the orchard, sending Matadin to one side and leaving the chief standing under the tree.

7

A Time of Loyalty

Ms Alice Harrison sat against a tree while her Indian servant went towards the well, with a box tucked under his arm. The other Indian servants were also near the well. Riyaz peeked from behind a tree to see the lay of the land and then quickly went to Alice. She was deep in thought, but as soon as she heard the crackling of leaves she looked up and, on seeing Riyaz, was both shocked and happy. 'Riyaz,' she exclaimed without thinking.

'Yes, it's Riyaz. You recognized me,' Riyaz replied as he came closer to her.

'Oh, Riyaz . . . Mr Riyaz . . .' she blurted out and suddenly stood up. 'What are you doing here?'

'Please sit down. Your knee is hurt,' said Riyaz as he looked at her.

'You . . .' Alice tried to say something.

'Look, you can speak to me as a friend. Please sit.'

Alice sat down and held on to her left knee.

'Are you badly hurt . . .?'

'Yes, it is hurting a lot,' she said with a painful expression on her face. 'But how did you find out? Are you staying here?'

'No,' replied Riyaz, 'I just got here this morning.'

In the meantime, two Indian soldiers marched up to Riyaz and asked threateningly, 'What's the matter? What are you doing here?'

Riyaz still had on the kurta pyjama and looked like a villager. Alice said to the two soldiers, 'I asked for him. You can go.'

'Your Ladyship, the major has ordered us not to allow anyone into the orchard.'

'I will tell Major Sahib. This man comes to the Residency sometimes.'

The two soldiers looked Riyaz up and down suspiciously and left.

'Have you even put any medicine on your wound?'

'I just applied some and tied this bandage.'

'If the pain has not lessened, I can bring some desi medicines,' Riyaz said as he sat down in front of her. 'I can find the medicines in this village.'

'Thank you,' Alice replied, gazing at him. 'What a coincidence that I met you again here.'

'I saw you when you were on your way to the hunt.'

'Fate wanted us to meet again, that is why I slipped and fell.'

'I was surprised to see you here. Just a few days ago there was fighting here, and the English are being killed everywhere.'

Alice stared at him intently and said, 'Riyaz, you too are in danger.'

'I know, but the most important thing for me is to discharge my duties.'

'We have also come here for this reason. I know that you are an officer of the rebel forces . . . but . . . but . . . Riyaz!' Her tone suddenly changed and she stuttered, 'Look, you must leave from here. Sir Henry Lawrence is sending his informants out. That is why my brother John Harrison and the others have come here.'

'So the hunt is just an excuse?'

'Yes. I shouldn't have told you, but I cannot lie to you.'

Riyaz immediately asked, 'So will you tell me whatever I ask you?'

Embarrassed, Alice looked at him longingly. Riyaz looked into her eyes and said, 'Alice, don't worry. I won't make it awkward for you.'

'Riyaz, don't test me,' she pleaded.

'Don't worry, Alice,' Riyaz replied as he got up. 'I am not going to take advantage of your good nature and your feelings.'

'Why did you stand up?' Alice asked worriedly.

'I am going . . .'

'Where?'

'Where I need to go. Your path and mine go in opposite directions.'

'Sit down.'

'No, Alice. Let me go. I have reached where I need to, so don't tie my hands now.'

'Can't we find a middle path?' Alice asked.

'No,' replied Riyaz. 'There is only one way left for the English and the Indians, and that is war. If the English and the Indians can now meet anywhere, it is on the battlefield.'

Alice sighed and asked, 'Riyaz, do you hate my people?'

'No, I am a friend of yours and your people. I am a friend of every human being,' Riyaz tried to explain to her. 'You are proof of this. But despite my actions, your people arrested me in Lucknow and humiliated me. You know what they wanted to do to me.'

'I am aware of their hypocrisy, and when I think of their actions I feel truly ashamed.'

'You freed me from the firangi prison, and for this I am eternally grateful.'

'Riyaz,' exclaimed Alice with shocked eyes. 'I didn't free you from prison to earn your gratitude.'

Changing the subject, Riyaz asked, 'So, what happened there after I left?'

'In the morning, when the chief commissioner found out that you had escaped, he sent search parties in all directions, and the native soldiers, who were guarding the Residency, were sent to Mandiaown.'

'But no one was suspicious of you?'

'No . . .'

'If I hadn't seen you here today, I would have sent someone to the Residency to find out about your well-being.'

'Really?'

'Yes!'

'Oh, Riyaz,' said Alice joyously. 'You are so kind and thoughtful to care for me like this.'

Riyaz turned towards the Indian soldiers. Four were sitting on the edge of the well, while four others were pacing about with their rifles. The servants were preparing food. Alice followed Riyaz's gaze and asked, 'Had the chief commissioner or the officers suspected me, what would you have done?'

'I would have freed you from their prison.'

'And had you not escaped from prison, had some officer arrested me when I was in that room with you, then what would you have done?'

'My comrades would have freed me by morning.'

'There would have been a lot of bloodshed.' Alice's face was overcome by fear.

'I know. I also know that if we were to attack the Residency right now, we would be victorious. But we haven't received orders yet.'

'Whose orders?' Alice asked immediately. 'Do you want to reinstate your king?'

'This War of Independence has nothing to do with the king. If the king had been capable, the British wouldn't have been able to conquer our country. The king's relatives, companions and the prime minister have made him a puppet—a mere figurehead.'

'So then, who is your leader?'

'You still don't know, do you?'

'No,' Alice replied in an innocent voice.

Riyaz read her face and said, 'Have you heard the name Maulvi Ahmadullah Shah?'

Alice's face turned pale.

'Arré! You have turned white!' Riyaz said, shocked. 'What's the matter, Alice? Why have you become so frightened on hearing Maulvi Sahib's name?'

'I have heard he is very cruel,' Alice said in a shaky voice.

'Well, that is completely false,' Riyaz said emphatically. 'It is British propaganda. He has ordered us to only fight those who fight us and to give refuge to those who seek it.'

'But . . .' Alice began to say something.

'No but-vut! It is true that some Indians have killed women and children, fed up with the cruelty of the firangis. This has happened because people want revenge. My troop's Major Doran* shot ten Indian soldiers without any provocation and was killed. If we wanted, we could have killed his wife, but I personally delivered her safely to Captain Forbes.† He took her to Lucknow. She is still in the Residency, and you can ask her if you like.'

'Yes, Mrs Doran told me about her children being saved, but I didn't know you were the one who saved them.'

'You will be surprised to hear that she was among those who identified me at the Residency and told Lawrence that I was a traitorous officer from the mutineering army.'

---

* Major Doran was the commander of the 10th Irregular Awadh Infantry. He was stationed with his troops in Sitapur. The major was a cruel man, and as soon as the War of Independence started, he was killed for revenge.

† On hearing about Indian soldiers' refusal to follow orders in Sitapur, Sir Henry Lawrence dispatched Captain Forbes from Lucknow with cavalrymen. They also took some wagons and rescued around fifteen English women and their children from Sitapur.

Alice bowed her head and started fiddling with her nails. Riyaz couldn't stop staring at her beautiful face. Seeing her embarrassed and ashamed, Riyaz said, 'You don't need to be ashamed. Why are you ashamed? I know you!'

'Riyaz,' Alice said, looking at him wistfully. 'Can this war not end?'

'Only if the angrez stay here as traders.'

Alice replied, 'But they shed their blood to conquer this country.'

'I am sorry, Alice. You don't know what is really happening. The angrez have used deception in every war they have fought. After the Battle of Buxar,★ they thought they became rulers of north India, but they deceived the Indians in that war. Then, in 1801, after the agreement, they set up cantonments everywhere and started to weaken the local rulers.'

'Listen, my family and I are against the current ways of the Company, but what can we do?'

'Tell your brothers to return to England,' Riyaz answered. 'Also give the others this advice. Your people will suffer because of the way Lawrence is behaving.'

The village chief was still standing under the tree, and as Riyaz glanced at him, he said to Alice, 'You must give me permission to leave. I shouldn't stay here for too long.'

Alice gazed at him with yearning and asked, 'When will we meet again?'

★ After the famous Battle of Buxar, the English became more entrenched in northern India and started their machinations in Awadh.

'I shall be in the city tonight.'

'It's too dangerous for you there.'

'I need to get some information.'

'Can I help you in any way?'

'Alice, you can do a lot for us . . .' But before finishing his sentence, he went quiet.

Alice said, 'Riyaz, trust me. I am not going to betray you, and I am ready to help in any way possible.'

'Alice!' Riyaz almost shouted in excitement.

'Yes, Riyaz. Believe me. You are such an exemplary young man—a true patriot. You are brave, and your actions will be remembered for generations to come. You are a hero for your people.'

'Alice, please, for God's sake, don't embarrass me,' Riyaz said to her softly. 'I haven't done anything yet. There is much to do.'

'Let me help you,' Alice said passionately. 'Think of me as loyal to you, not the English. Riyaz, I cannot bring myself to tell you what I think of you.' Overcome by emotions, she took his hands into hers.

'Alice, the soldiers are coming over here,' Riyaz whispered with a sense of urgency.

Alice let go of his hands. Two Indian soldiers came up to them, and one of them said to Alice, 'Miss Baba! He should not be here for so long. If the major sees him with you, we will get into a lot of trouble.'

'The major knows this man and respects him a lot,' Alice replied.

'You can go. I just wanted some company, so I asked him to sit. He is just leaving.'

When both the soldiers had left, Riyaz said to Alice, 'I shouldn't stay here much longer.'

Alice asked him again, 'Why are you going to Lucknow?'

'I need to find out where Sir Henry Lawrence has stashed his magazine.'

'In Machchi Bhawan. Is that all you wanted to know?'

'I know this. I need to find out where exactly in Machchi Bhawan.'

'Hmm. I don't know, but I am willing to find out for you.'

'Alice!' exclaimed Riyaz. 'Am I dreaming?'

'What's there to dream about?'

'Can an English lady give away the secrets of her people to the enemy?'

'You are not my enemy . . . In fact . . . Riyaz . . .' Her voice seemed stuck in her throat as she gazed at him lovingly.

'Alice,' exclaimed Riyaz, this time nervously. 'What is this? What am I hearing?'

'My heart's desire,' Alice immediately replied. 'It is the sound of my heart. Can you hear it, Riyaz?'

'Yes, Alice, I can hear your heart beating. I see . . .'

'I shall find out everything about the magazine from Captain James.'

'Should I come to the Residency tonight?'

'How can you come there?' asked Alice.

'Don't worry about that. I got arrested that day because I wasn't careful,' said Riyaz.

'If you enter the Residency through the southern gate, you will find me waiting for you in the veranda of the first building. I shall call the soldiers and explain.'

'I shall reach by nine o'clock.'

'I will be in the garden near the gate.'

The village chief was standing under the mahua tree, fiddling with his turban. Riyaz got up and looked into Alice's eyes. 'Khuda hafiz, Alice.'

Alice looked at him, holding back tears. Her red lips were trembling. Riyaz quickly headed out of the orchard and into the path. The chief went around the outskirts and motioned to him to head towards the village.

Riyaz wound his way past the thatched roofs and slatted awnings and stopped in front of a Shivalay. The chief was right behind him. He called out to Riyaz to stop and, getting closer, he asked, 'Jamadar Sahib, the officers are on their way back. Matadin sent Ajodhya. He says they are very close.'

'That's why I left.'

'Did that madam say anything, though?'

'No, she won't say anything,' Riyaz explained to the chief. 'If anyone asks, you say a mian sahib from Lucknow came from Malhor and went towards Lucknow.'

'Is there anything to be frightened of?' asked the chief.

'Well, we don't need to be scared of them, but perhaps we should be frightened of you.'

'But, Jamadar Sahib, I am one of you.'

'Yes, but you are so nervous that you might give away everything.'

Embarrassed, the chief said, 'No, this can never happen, even if I die.'

'Good. Bring me my horse. I shall wait here.'

The chief asked, 'Will you leave right away?'

'No,' replied Riyaz. 'But I need to disappear from here. Hide my clothes, all right?'

The chief went to fetch the horse. Riyaz cupped his hands and drank some water from a well near the Shivalay and wiped his face. He had been pacing to and fro when the chief appeared with the horse.

'Have the firangis reached the orchard?'

'Not yet, but they are on this side of the *barsaati naala*.'

Riyaz patted his horse on the neck and said to the chief, 'Firstly, the firangis won't ask you anything. If they do, remember what I told you about the mian sahib returning from Malhor to Lucknow. You cannot be nervous or frightened, or you will get into trouble, as will the others. If you want to help us, there is no scope for fear. I shall return after two hours.'

Riyaz mounted his horse and headed out of the village.

8

A Conference between Three Leaders

As promised, Riyaz returned after two hours. On asking if the firangis had left, the chief said, 'Matadin heard one of the Indian soldiers telling a firangi that someone had come to see the memsahib.'

'Then what happened?' asked Riyaz.

Matadin arrived, and Riyaz asked him for the details.

'One of the Indian soldiers said to the major that a man came and sat next to the memsahib and chatted with her. The major asked the memsahib something in English, and then they started talking among themselves.'

'Did they get angry with her?'

'Not at all. She said something and they all started laughing.'

The chief said to Matadin, 'Go, tie Jamadar Sahib's horse under the village pavilion and give it some grass.'

Matadin left. The chief put a charpoy on the platform in front of the house, and Riyaz sat down on it.

After some time, Riyaz took a bath and said to the chief, 'Can Sheikh Ji lend me these clothes until tomorrow?'

'Yes, of course. Take them, I shall inform him.'

Matadin came and asked, 'Jamadar Sahib, what should be cooked for you. If you like, some meat can be cooked at Sheikh Ji's house.'

'Bhai, don't worry. I am leaving shortly. So don't have any food prepared.'

Riyaz offered his dusk prayers, tied up his uniform in a bundle and rode towards Muhibullahpur. He saw some Indian cavalrymen near Ismailganj. They were going towards Mudkipur. Riyaz went through the fields, avoiding them, and reached Muhibullahpur after an hour.

Raja Nawab Ali Sahib had already reached and was sitting at the house of a zamindar called Habib Ahmad. Riyaz sent word that he had come, and Raja Sahib immediately called him in. Sitting next to him was Azeemullah Khan.★ Raja Sahib introduced Riyaz to him and said, 'This is the man I just mentioned to you . . .'

Azeemullah Khan shook Riyaz's hand, and the three started to talk. Riyaz gave Raja Sahib the subedar's letter

---

★ Historical accounts and books tell us that Azeemullah Khan came to Lucknow a number of times and conferred with the leaders of the War of Independence. Maulvi Hameedullah Khan was an elder who lived near the *towpkhanah*. He died at the age of 110 in 1934. Khan Mahboob Tarzi had the opportunity to meet him dozens of times. He often used to speak of the mutiny and would mention General Azeemullah Khan, with whom he was stationed in Kanpur for six or seven months. Maulvi Hameedullah Khan's son, Majeedullah Khan, had passed away by the time of the writing of this novel. He was an inspector in the telegraph department. His family now lives in Maulviganj.

and told him about the situation in Nawabganj. Raja Jai Lal Singh also arrived. He embraced Riyaz and said, 'Riyaz Mian, I congratulate you on your successful escape. If you hadn't escaped from the Residency that night, we would have been forced to attack the next day.'

Raja Nawab Ali Sahib said, 'It's good that we were not forced to attack, otherwise we would have had to fight before the time was right. I only found out about your arrest and escape today.'

Riyaz told him the details of his arrest and escape. He also repeated whatever Henry Lawrence had told him. Raja Sahib said, 'In any case, don't budge on your principles. Whoever asks for refuge should be granted it. Lawrence's plans will be foiled and he will be killed very soon. The cruelty he has inflicted on Indians will not be forgotten by history.'

'Without a doubt,' Azeemullah Khan exclaimed. 'There is no limit to his cruelty.'

Suddenly, Raja Jai Lal Singh spoke up, 'He has crossed all limits. Twenty-five of your soldiers escorted six angrez here, and that bastard had them all hanged.'

'It's no problem,' Raja Nawab Ali Sahib said. 'The seed of freedom must be watered with blood. One day, those innocent people's blood will give colour to this land.'

Azeemullah Khan said, 'Those tyrants did not even pause to think that these soldiers are the very people who saved their English compatriots.'

Riyaz said, 'Lawrence thinks very highly of himself and his capabilities.'

'He's deluded,' Raja Nawab Ali said angrily. 'He must be proud of his duplicity and of how he breaks oaths. He doesn't know what humanity and civility mean.'

Raja Jai Lal Singh said, 'We will turn his arrogance into dust.'

Azeemullah Khan turned towards Raja Jai Lal Singh and asked, 'What have you thought of doing about the magazine?'

'My man must have reached Mallanvaan*, and from there via Fatehgarh and Farrukhabad he will go to Qaimganj. As soon as he reaches, he will send the magazines.'

'The angrez have lots of magazines in Lucknow,' Raja Nawab Ali said. 'I have heard that Lawrence has shifted the magazine from Dar-e-Daulat to Machchi Bhawan.'

'You are absolutely right,' Riyaz replied. 'But we still do not know the exact building in Machchi Bhawan in which the magazine has been stored.'

'It is imperative to find out,' Raja Jai Lal Singh said with urgency. 'There are a few houses in Daryaee Tola and Sibtainabad that have underground tunnels to Machchi Bhawan. We can use those tunnels to get in and take away the magazines.'

Azeemullah Khan said, 'If we get our hands on their magazines, we shall be able to push the firangis all the way to Calcutta.'

---

* Mallanvaan was a district of Khairabad division. The deputy commissioner lived there, as did soldiers, to guard the government treasury. It was a bustling and well-to-do town and people going to Delhi went via Mallanvaan. Raja Narpat Singh of Ruiya Garhi and his men beat back the English twice from a spot near the town. The town was completely ruined and is now nothing more than a small village.

'My spies are prepared,' said Raja Jai Lal Singh. 'But they still have not been able to find out which building the magazine is in. Lawrence has put a heavy guard there.'

Raja Nawab Ali and Azeemullah Khan both lowered their heads and pondered over this matter. The Indians had a shortage of cannonballs and gunpowder.

Seeing them worried, Riyaz said, 'Please do not worry. By tonight I shall have all the information about the magazines.'

'And how is that?' Raja Nawab Ali Khan said to Riyaz in a surprised voice.

'I will enter the Residency after nine o'clock.'

'Mian Riyaz Ahmad Khan! This is a very dangerous game,' said Raja Nawab Ali. 'Sir Henry Lawrence and his dogs are out to catch your scent. They are everywhere. You managed to escape their custody, and this is not to be taken lightly.'

'You are completely right, but please don't worry. The magazine has been stored in the cellars under the supervision of Captain James.'

'How will you get this information from him?' asked Raja Jai Lal Singh.

'The information must have been obtained from him by now.'

Raja Nawab Ali interjected, 'Please tell me who might have obtained this information.'

'Ms Alice Harrison,' Riyaz said with some hesitation. 'She and I met this afternoon in an orchard near Chinhat.'

'I suppose this is the same firangi girl who helped you escape prison,' said Raja Nawab Ali.

'Yes! She has promised this today and will wait for me tonight at nine o'clock near the Residency's gate,' said Riyaz.

'Are you sure you won't be tricked?' Raja Jai Lal Singh asked.

'No question of it. I am sure.'

Azeemullah Khan said with a wry smile, 'A lady cannot play a trick on such a strapping and brave young man.'

Raja Nawab Ali said, 'Good. Then go tonight. It is already eight.'

Riyaz greeted Raja Nawab Ali, Raja Jai Lal Singh and Azeemullah Khan. As he was about to leave, Raja Nawab Ali said, 'I would have left tonight, but I shall wait for your return. You are entering the hornet's nest. May God keep you safe in His protection.'

Riyaz bade them farewell, went outside and mounted his horse. He reached Takiya Pir Jalal via the Pukka Pul. After entrusting his horse to a friend, he reached the southern gate of the Residency. Four Indian soldiers were pacing to and fro with rifles. One of them shouted, 'Stop! Who goes there?'

'A servant,' replied Riyaz.

The soldier straightened his rifle and asked, 'Where are you going?'

'To Major Harrison's house.'

'Let him go,' the other soldier interjected. 'He has brought medicine for Miss Baba. She just told me that he was coming.'

Riyaz entered the Residency and went past the gates. Someone was walking in the garden. He approached the figure cautiously. Alice recognized him from his gait and whispered, 'Riyaz?'

'Yes, it's me.'

'Come over here. To the right.'

Riyaz couldn't see anything. So he fumbled in the dark and reached a bed of flowers. He looked here and there.

'Come further,' Alice's voice came through the darkness. 'This is a safe place.'

Riyaz reached her. Alice took his hands into her own and whispered, 'Riyaz, you came.'

'Yes, Alice,' replied Riyaz quietly. 'Why wouldn't I come? After all, I promised you.'

Alice heaved a sigh of relief and put both her hands on his shoulders.

'Alice,' Riyaz quietly called out to her in the darkness.

'Ye . . . ye . . . yes,' replied Alice.

Riyaz put his hands on her shoulders and whispered in her left ear, 'What's the matter, Alice?'

'Will we ever meet like this again?'

'What happens tomorrow, only God knows. We should keep our eyes on the present. Alice, I am in the middle of the enemy camp. I shouldn't stay here for long.'

Alice was startled. She took a step back and looked around. 'The magazine is in the middle building.'

'In the cellars?'

'Yes,' replied Alice. 'But it has a heavy guard around it.'

'Alice, how can I ever thank you?'

'Do you still want to thank me?' Alice asked him.

'I am very close to my goal, Alice. Please don't stop me from going further.'

'But I am lost, Riyaz. You need to help me,' Alice pleaded as she hugged him and started to sob.

Riyaz drew her head into his chest and hugged her tightly, his fingers caressing her hair. 'What are you saying, Alice? You know the position I am in.'

Alice sobbed, 'Yes, yes. I know. Fine, you should go now.'

'Are you upset?'

'No, Riyaz. How can I be upset with you?' Alice said, trying to control her sobbing. 'I am honestly and happily telling you to go, but remember me. My life is yours.'

Riyaz hugged her even more closely and pressed her head into his chest. 'Allow me to go now,' he said as he stroked her back.

'Go . . . Khuda hafiz.'

Alice was not able to ask him when they would meet next.

Riyaz quickly left the Residency. The streets were empty. He went through an alley and paused under a tree. There were some people standing at the corner, talking. He stared at them for a while and then went into another alley. He entered his friend's house, mounted his horse and rode towards Muhibullahpur.

Near Shah Naseeruddin's Karbala, he noticed a coach heading towards the city, accompanied by four armed riders. Riyaz recognized the coach from a distance. He motioned to the coachman to stop. Raja Jai Lal Singh also recognized him and called out to him.

As soon as Riyaz reached him, he dismounted and bowed down to offer his salaam. Azeemullah Khan was sitting next to Raja Jai Lal Singh.

Raja Jai Lal Singh asked Riyaz, 'Is everything alright?'

'Yes,' replied Riyaz.

'What did you find out?'

'It is in the basement of the middle building.'

'Well done!' Raja Jai Lal Singh exclaimed as he climbed down from the coach and embraced Riyaz. Azeemullah Khan also dismounted and patted Riyaz on the back.

'Riyaz Ahmad Khan Sahib, you have solved a very important problem through your efforts.'

'I am just an ordinary soldier with the army that is trying to free the country from slavery. My duty is to follow your orders.'

Raja Jai Lal Singh said, 'Raja Sahib Mahmudabad is waiting for you. Go quickly, so that he can leave by morning. If you have time, come and see me later.'

Riyaz talked for a little longer and then left to meet Raja Nawab Ali Khan Sahib.

Raja Sahib was talking to his host, Habeeb Ahmad Sahib, when he saw Riyaz. He stood up, went towards Riyaz and embraced him. He then looked towards the heavens and said, 'Thank God. Thank God a thousand times.'

He immediately took out five ashrafis from his pocket, held them to Riyaz's forehead and gave them to Habeeb Ahmad, saying, 'Distribute these among the poor tomorrow.'

Habeeb Ahmad came forward and took the gold. Raja Sahib made Riyaz sit next to him and was debriefed about the situation. He said, 'Good. Now you come with me to Mahmudabad.'

'Your wish is my command,' Riyaz said gratefully. 'But I am needed in Nawabganj.'

'Our troops are under the command of the subedar.'

'Yes, but there is no one in Nawabganj who can easily go to Lucknow.'

'It's not a good idea for you to go again and again to Lucknow.'

'Yes, you are right. But it is also important for me to discharge my duties.'

'Riyaz, may God protect you and make you succeed in your plans. You are definitely right. Not everyone can do what you are doing!'

Riyaz bowed to offer his salaam. Raja Sahib said, 'This country will be freed by brave and great young men like you, and Mahmudabad's name will be written in the history of independent India in golden letters.'

Riyaz lowered his head. Habib Ahmad approached Raja Sahib with folded hands and asked, 'Your Highness, if you permit, dinner can be served.'

'Yes. Riyaz has returned, and now I shall eat.'

As Habeeb Ahmad left, Riyaz asked, 'Has Your Highness not had his dinner yet?'

'Riyaz, I had made an oath to myself that I would not eat until you returned from the Residency. If, God forbid, you had been arrested, then a force of 10,000 men from the city would have attacked the Residency.'

'This is not the time for that,' Riyaz replied. 'Until we have artillery, we won't really be able to make a dent in the firangi forces.'

'This is what I was telling Raja Jai Lal Singh and Azeemullah Khan. Anyway, it's a matter of a few days now. I trust Shah Sahib and know that he will not hold back in fighting these criminals.'

Habeeb Ahmad arrived and said, 'Your Highness, dinner has been laid out.'

9

Unrest in the Residency

Sir Henry Lawrence thought that the preparations he had made were enough to keep the government safe in north India. More than trusting his artillery and his firangi and native forces, he trusted his army of spies. Kannauji Lal and others like him had persuaded Sir Lawrence that the mutineering Indian armies and armed civilians would not be able to do anything to the angrez. It was these very traitors who had also assured Lawrence that they knew all the secrets of the rebel army but the mutineers did not know their secrets. However, on 22 June, Sir Henry Lawrence was disabused of this notion.

Early in the morning, Captain James came in a nervous state to see the chief commissioner. As soon as he arrived, he said, 'There is a big problem. The Indians know about the cellars in which we have hidden the magazines.'

'What are you saying, James?' Lawrence asked curtly.

'What I have seen with my own eyes. Last night, some armed civilians managed to reach the magazine but luckily

Private James also went into the cellars in a drunken stupor and heard their footsteps. He started shouting and raised the alarm and so they ran away.'

'How is it possible that, despite such a heavy guard, these blighters found their way in?' asked Lawrence pointedly.

'It shouldn't be possible but it was and here is proof of it,' James said as he reached into his pocket, took out a white badge and placed it on the desk. 'Look at this. There are two fish on this badge that form a circle. It is a symbol of the city folk who are with the mutineers.'

Lawrence picked up the badge, looked at it for a few seconds and said, 'You found this in the cellars?'

'Yes, and if you remember, the city kotwal handed a similar badge to you.'

'Hmm, I remember. This means that if we are not careful, the mutineers will either steal the magazine or destroy it.'

'Yes, this is what I think too.'

'Very well, then. Station twenty soldiers of the 32nd Regiment inside the cellars.'

'Very good, sir.'

'And also start bringing the magazine here. If I had known that place was not safe, I would have ordered for it to be brought to the Residency.'

Captain James stood up, as did Sir Lawrence who walked around the desk. His brow was furrowed and then, his hands in his pockets, he said, 'The question is, how did those criminals get in there?'

'There are a number of tunnels that go from Machchi Bhawan into the city and there are dozens of people who know their way around them. They must have used those tunnels.'

'Yes, that seems likely but then the other question is, how did the mutineers know that the magazine was in the middle building's cellars?'

'Their spies keep coming here.'

'But only a few officers know about it. You didn't mention it in passing to anyone, did you?'

'No, sir,' James immediately replied. 'I think our spies are traitors.'

'Yes, that might be the case,' Lawrence said as he paced up and down his room. 'I myself don't trust those dogs but what can we do, as things stand?'

Captain James was about to leave when Lawrence stopped him and said, 'The information about the magazine wasn't acquired by the mutineers through an Indian.'

'Then who was it?'

'I shall tell you by the afternoon.'

Captain James saluted him and left.

In the afternoon, Sir Henry Lawrence called him back and said, 'I just found out from Macmillan that a few days ago, when Major Harrison and some others went out of the city, Ms Alice stayed back in an orchard all alone.'

'But Macmillan told me that Ms Alice had slipped and fallen and had stayed back.'

'That's what he told me. But she stayed there for an hour and a half to two hours alone, and in that time, an Indian came to see her and spoke to her for a long time.'

'Have you asked Ms Harrison about this?'

'Not yet. I have not asked her anything but I shall call for her now.'

He wrote something on a piece of paper and called for a peon. Giving the peon the paper, he said, 'House of Major Harrison, do you know it?'

'Yes, Your Excellency.'

'There you'll find Miss Baba, give her this paper and convey my greetings.'

The peon left and Alice arrived after fifteen minutes, carrying a book in her hand. Lawrence stood up to greet her. She sat down and he sat on a chair facing her.

'Ms Harrison, I have heard that when you went on the hunt the day before yesterday you fell and hurt yourself?'

'Yes, I hurt my knee and that is why I returned.'

'To the orchard?'

'Yes.'

'There, did an Indian man visit you?'

'He didn't visit me but was passing through,' Alice replied without hesitating. 'He had seen me a number of times in the Residency, so he recognized me and came to talk to me.'

'And what, pray, did he say to you?'

'He must have seen me tying a bandage on my knee and came to ask if I was all right.'

'Do you know him?' Captain James asked.

'No, but I have seen him a number of times.'

'I heard that he sat and talked to you for nearly an hour,' said Lawrence.

'Yes, it was hot, so he sat in the shade and told me hunting tales.'

'The Indian soldiers who accompanied you described his appearance, and it matches that of Riyaz Ahmad Khan.'

'That man was dressed like a poor Muslim villager.'

'Riyaz Ahmad Khan is an extremely dangerous mutineer,' interjected Lawrence, 'and Macmillan tells me that you were quite taken up by him.'

'Riyaz Ahmad Khan saved our lives and we should all be grateful to him. If Mr Macmillan does not feel this way, then he is an ingrate.'

Lawrence looked at Alice Harrison in amazement as she continued speaking, 'I want to ask you, should we not be grateful for that act of his?'

'It is true that he saved seven English lives and one of them was you but that does not change the fact that he is a mutineer.'

Alice changed her tone and said, 'In any case, I don't need to think about these matters. I often see the man I met in the orchard in the Residency and the next time I spot him, I shall let you know.'

'Ms Harrison,' Lawrence said firmly, 'perhaps you should think about this once more.'

'Think about what?' asked Alice.

'Whether or not that man was Riyaz Ahmad Khan.'

'You have seen Riyaz Ahmad Khan and when that man returns to the Residency, you can see for yourself,' said Alice sarcastically. 'It is unfortunate that I am being suspected because of Macmillan's statements.'

Captain James said, 'Nowadays, we don't even trust our own shadows.'

'That's not healthy,' replied Alice, 'and this is what is referred to as superstition.'

She started to smile. Lawrence angrily said, 'You are smiling even though the mutineers have killed more than 250 men, women, old people and children!'

Instead of replying, Alice looked away, staring at the greenery outside. After a few minutes, Lawrence said, 'Ms Alice Harrison, you are free to go.'

'Thank you,' said Alice as she got up.

She glanced at Captain James and left. After she had gone, Sir Henry looked at the Captain and said, 'What a strange girl.'

'I used to think so too but from her views, it seems that she is quite serious and dignified,' said Captain James.

'Not just dignified but also resolute,' said Sir Henry. 'She kept defending Riyaz Ahmad Khan right till the end.'

'Why don't you call for Major Harrison and speak to him?'

'He too has a similar disposition,' Lawrence replied.

Macmillan entered the room and, as he took off his cap, he said, 'I was told by a sentry that the day we went hunting, a man of a similar description entered the Residency through the southern gate.'

'Whom did he go to see?'

'I didn't ask the sentry this.'

'Well, come back after finding out then.'

Macmillan left and returned after ten minutes with two native sentries. They both saluted and stood at attention. Lawrence turned to one of them and asked, 'Did someone come in two nights ago through the southern gate?'

'Yes, a man wearing kurta, pyjama and a saafa.'

'With whose permission did you allow him to enter?'

'Your Excellency, Miss Baba had said that a man would bring her medicine and that he should be allowed in.'

'Which Miss Baba . . .?'

'The one who lives with Major Sahib,' replied the sentry.

The other sentry confirmed this story and Lawrence dismissed them. He turned to Macmillan and said, 'You can go too.'

As soon as Macmillan left, Lawrence said, 'James, the entire matter seems very complicated. I believe that Ms Harrison is in love with that young Indian chap, Riyaz Ahmad Khan. He met her in the orchard in Chinhat during the day and then at night here.'

'You are absolutely right,' replied Captain James. 'And the secret of where our magazines are was revealed to the Indians by Ms Alice Harrison.'

'Does she know about the magazines?'

'Yes. That very evening Ms Harrison had spoken to me about the magazines and during the course of our conversation, I told her that it was stored in the cellar of the middle building.'

Sir Henry Lawrence closed his eyes, leaned back, put his head on the chair's headrest and paused to think for a while. He then leaned forward and said, 'You made a mistake, Captain James, but you acknowledged it, which is satisfactory. Speak to Ms Harrison again this evening . . .'

'What should I speak to her about?'

'Find out what her views are,' replied Lawrence. 'She is betraying her people because of her love for an Indian. She can turn out to be very dangerous.'

'She should be sent away from here.'

'All the roads are closed. Where can she be sent?' Lawrence asked James.

'Yes, she cannot be sent outside Lucknow. She should be put under house arrest in the Residency.'

'That won't be a wise move,' replied Lawrence. 'Major John Harrison will become our enemy.'

Captain James stared at the floor pensively. Sir Henry said, 'I shall get to the bottom of this by the evening.'

'You should put her under watch straightaway.'

'Indeed. I shall call Colonel Forbes and explain the whole matter to him.'

Captain James left.

That evening after dinner, as Sir Henry was leaving the mess, Captain James stopped him and said, 'I need to tell you something.'

'Ah, yes. I was looking for you too. Tell me, what did you speak to Ms Harrison about?'

'Macmillan has told Ms Harrison everything. He's a complete oaf and is head over heels in love with her.'

'He could turn out to be more dangerous than Alice. Anyway, I shall take care of this too.'

As they neared Sir Henry's quarters, Captain James said, 'Ms Harrison is very shrewd. She didn't even speak about all this to me.'

'Right. Well, you go and bring the magazine back to the Residency.'

Captain James about-turned and left.

The next morning, Sir Henry called Ms Harrison back to his office. He repeated everything the sentries had told him and asked, 'What do you have to say for yourself?'

'Why don't you enquire, then I shall answer you!'

'Ms Harrison, perhaps you are unaware what the penalty is for treason?'

'I am completely aware, Your Excellency,' she said in a raised voice, 'but I am not used to being spoken to like this. If you suspect me, have me put under house arrest straightaway. Otherwise, I shall take your leave.'

'You seem very agitated . . .'

'Please do not make me get into a conversation about personal matters,' Alice exclaimed. 'I do not wish to speak to you about any of this.'

'Are you aware that it is a matter of life and death for us in this country? Scores of Englishmen have been killed already.'

'Would you like to know my opinion about this?'

'Not at all,' replied the wiry Englishman. 'All I am saying is, do not get carried away by your present circumstances and cause incalculable and inexcusable damage to our people.'

'Well then, Your Excellency should have me thrown into prison right away.'

Sir Henry glared at her. Alice continued to speak, 'Keeping the circumstances in mind, you should not give anyone any leeway.'

'I did not call you here for advice,' he replied. 'You may leave now.'

'Thank you!' Alice said tersely and quickly left the office.

Outside, Mrs Doran was coming from the direction of the treasury. She saw Alice leaving Lawrence's office and walked over. Sir Henry saw her and went outside.

'Mrs Doran, do you wish to tell me something?'

'Yes. That young lady who left your office is in love with a young Indian man.'

'And how do you know of this?'

'From Macmillan,' she replied. 'He has told everyone about this.'

'He is an idiot,' retorted Lawrence.

'I know, but the young man she loves is really very brave and handsome. If he were to wear European clothes, no one would be able to tell him apart from us.'

'Mrs Doran, please try and reason with Alice Harrison. She will set a very bad example and he will continue to obtain our secrets through her.'

'Yes, this is what I think too. She's a rash young girl. What does she understand of these matters?'

She put Lawrence's heart to rest and walked off grumbling to herself. He went back into his office.

10

Alice under Suspicion

Rumour was rife about the arrival of the native forces from Nawabganj. Very early in the afternoon, the subedar of Riyaz's platoon called him and said, 'Maulvi Sahib has called over the officers and told them about some important matters. Tomorrow we shall leave and day after, we enter Lucknow.'

'What are my orders? Should I remain with my platoon?'

'No. You should leave with 200 cavalrymen right away and make sure that they are able to get into the city before the afternoon tomorrow.'

'They will be in the city before the afternoon tomorrow, sir.'

'From which side will you enter the city?'

'From Madhee,' replied Riyaz. 'We have loyal men in the village and some reasonably good boats too. We can easily transport a few thousand men into the city from there.'

'Right. Why don't you go and eat?' said the subedar. 'And just before you leave, I shall share some important information with you.'

Riyaz left and returned after an hour. The subedar called him into his tent and spoke to him for a while before sending him off. Riyaz came out, inspected the troops, said goodbye to his friends and set off. After riding for two hours, they rested near a lake and, just after the sunset prayers, they reached a large opening in Madhee. The moon had still not appeared and Riyaz stopped his soldiers and said, 'Take off your uniforms and wear civilian clothes. I'll be right back.'

He went towards the town and, after half an hour, returned along with two men. One of the soldiers walked up to him and asked, 'Can we cook here?'

'No,' Riyaz immediately replied, 'food has been prepared for all of you and two riders will reach here by eight o'clock.'

Another soldier interjected, 'Did the villagers prepare food for us?'

'No, Raja Sahib has organized a bawarchikhana and a bhandara here so that our soldiers who are fighting for freedom need not worry about food and water.'*

One of the villagers addressed the soldier, saying, 'Food will be brought here by cart so you can just eat where you are.'

---

* Bawarchikhanas and bhandaras would have provided food for Muslims and Hindus respectively. In a largely religious society, care was taken to keep in mind the beliefs of people as well as their dietary restrictions. Many Muslim rajas would call for the services of a local pandit to cook for Hindu guests, and separate crockery and cutlery was kept for them.

'In the dark?' asked someone.

'Yes. It is not a good idea to light torches as we are not far from La Martinière's bungalow and there are 500 soldiers stationed there.'

The soldiers settled down and, having eaten, they took boats and alighted on the other side of the river. Riyaz divided them into groups of eights and tens and, addressing all of them, said, 'You should all take separate paths into the city and wait for us at Sarai Agha Mir.'

'Won't the police or the English spies suspect us?' asked one of the soldiers.

'No. Just don't act as if you are from out of town,' replied Riyaz.

Everyone went their separate ways. Riyaz went to Bagh-e-Qazi where he met with a leader of the freedom fighters, Mustapha Khan, and they both headed towards Sarai Agha Mir. Riyaz asked Mustapha Khan, 'Khan Sahib, do your men have any way of getting into the Residency?'

'Yes, there is a man called Mohan Shukla in the commissioner's office who gives me information. Apart from him, two of my most trusted men, Shiv Mangal and Qaim Reza, go in and out of the Residency without any problem.'

'I need to find out if Major John Harrison's sister, Ms Alice Harrison, is all right.'

'Tomorrow morning, before ten o'clock, you will get news of her.'

'That firangi lady helped me escape from prison and also informed me about the secret location of the magazine.'

'If Lawrence finds out, he will have her imprisoned.'

Riyaz remained silent and they reached Sarai Agha Mir. Riyaz's soldiers were arriving there in groups of twos and fours. Mustapha Khan turned to Riyaz, 'Please send fifty men to Raja Jai Lal Singh. Then station three groups of twenty-five men each in Sarai Darbijay Singh, Sarai Agha Mir and Garheywali Sarai. The rest of the men should be sent to me.'

Riyaz followed Mustapha Khan's orders, and then went to Mirza Haider Baig's place.

At eight o'clock, Mustapha Khan also arrived there and said, 'Shiv Mangal went to the Residency this morning and he is certain that Lawrence suspects Ms Harrison of disclosing the location of the magazine to you. He has called her to his office a number of times, but she has not told him anything. They are all very worried about her and see her as a traitor.'

Riyaz asked, 'Khan Sahib, is there any way we can smuggle Alice Harrison out of the Residency?'

'For the time being, it's not possible,' replied Mustapha Khan. 'There is a high alert, guards outside and inside the Residency.'

'What if they have imprisoned her?' asked Riyaz.

'In that case, the only option is to attack the Residency,' Mustapha Khan said, 'but it is only a matter of a day or two. Today, Maulvi Sahib will march towards Lucknow with his army.'

'Yes,' Riyaz said, deep in thought. 'In any case, I shall leave this afternoon and return during the day tomorrow.'

'You go, I will make sure my men keep track of Ms Harrison. Almost a quarter of the servants in the Residency are our men.'

Mirza Haider Baig also came out to talk. Riyaz said, 'If Maulvi Sahib reaches Chinhat, they will attack Lucknow the day after tomorrow.'

'Yes,' replied Mustapha Khan, 'that is what Maulvi Sahib said in his letter.'

Riyaz had lunch with them and left after half an hour.

Four Englishmen stopped him near Machchi Bhawan and an officer cantered up to them. As the Englishmen started speaking to each other, an Indian officer from the 7th Risala arrived. He had seen Riyaz imprisoned in the Residency and recognized him. Motioning to Riyaz with his eyes, he said out loud, 'Oh ho, Mirza Sahib, it's you. What brings you to these parts?'

Riyaz understood that the Indian officer was a freedom fighter and replied, 'I came to meet everyone.'

The English officer asked the Indian officer, 'Do you know this man?'

'Yes, sir. This is Naseerullah Baig's younger brother. You can see from his face.'

'You may go,' said the Englishman.

The Indian officer called out to Riyaz as he was leaving, 'Mirza Sahib, convey my salaam to everyone.'

Riyaz smiled, nodded and spurred his horse on.

The Indian armies had arrived at Malhor and had set up camp in a mango orchard. He went to his subedar, debriefed him about the situation and they went to meet Maulvi Ahmadullah Shah. He was sitting on a carpet under a tree, explaining tactics to some officers.

Riyaz sat down at the back of the group.

After a while, Maulvi Sahib dismissed the officers, called Riyaz and asked him about the situation in Lucknow. Riyaz told him everything and added, 'Ms Alice Harrison had informed me about the location of the magazine and Raja Jai Lal Singh's men reached there but were unable to capture it.'

'I know,' replied Maulvi Sahib, 'I received Raja Sahib's letter in Nawabganj. In any case, the magazine is still in Machchi Bhawan.'

'Yes, they were unable to move it till this afternoon,' said Riyaz, 'but Lawrence wants to move it to another location. We should attack by the day after at the latest. The firangis will leave Machchi Bhawan to defend the Residency, and we will be able to capture it.'

'I have informed our brave men and their leaders in Lucknow that when we move towards Lucknow, they should arm themselves and surround the Englishmen wherever they find them.'

'What are your orders for me?' asked Riyaz.

'You leave early in the morning tomorrow, and we shall leave in the afternoon so that we reach the orchards of Chinhat by the evening.'

'So should I come in the morning?'

'Yes,' replied Maulvi Sahib, 'if you get any important information, then definitely let me know.'

Riyaz walked over with the subedar to his soldiers. He spent the night there and left before daybreak for the city via Madhee. Mustapha Khan was stationing his men near the Residency and Machchi Bhawan. He took Riyaz into an alley and, checking to see if anyone else was there, said, 'Lawrence has found out that you were in the city yesterday. He has alerted his spies. It will be better if you go to my house and I shall join you there shortly.'

Riyaz dismounted from his horse and, navigating his way through small alleys, reached Mustapha Khan's house. After half an hour, Mustapha Khan also arrived and both of them talked about the situation.

Mustapha Khan said, 'Qaim Reza and Shiv Mangal have established contact with Ms Harrison through her bearer.'

'Really?' exclaimed Riyaz excitedly.

'Yes. The bearer's name is Kallan Khan and he is regularly in touch with both of them. Ms Harrison even spoke to Shiv Mangal and was asking after you.'

'Did they give you any new information?' asked Riyaz.

'This morning, they told me that Captain James has been bringing out cartons of cartridges from Machchi Bhawan.'

'You mean the magazine is being moved?'

'How much will they be able to move? Tomorrow we attack!'

'You're right. Tomorrow Raja Sahib will arrive with a force of 2000 as well as an army of Pasis,' replied Riyaz.

Mustapha Khan faced Riyaz and asked, 'What is your plan now?'

'I shall stay here, get all the information I can, and leave early tomorrow. Maulvi Sahib should reach Chinhat with his forces by this evening.'

Mustapha Khan said, 'Mirza Haider Baig has placed his informers among the villagers.'

'If you think it appropriate, could you ask Shiv Mangal and Qaim Reza to keep me informed about Ms Harrison and also to assure her that Lawrence will not be able to do anything to her?'

'You rest here. I am going in that direction. About two hours ago, I saw her near the southern gate. I think her mother was with her.'

'Please tell Shiv Mangal that he should keep meeting her.'

Mustapha Khan took him to another floor of the house and left him in a room. He returned in the afternoon and the two men had lunch together. After eating, Riyaz got up to leave and Mustapha Khan said, 'Shiv Mangal Singh has informed Ms Harrison that you are in the city.'

'Did she say anything?' asked Riyaz.

'She promised that she would send Shiv Mangal and Qaim Reza messages through Kallan Khan and keep them abreast of the situation.'

'Khan Sahib,' Riyaz exclaimed passionately, 'this firangi girl has really helped us a lot.'

'You're right. We have been able to find out Lawrence's secrets and her help has truly been invaluable.'

Riyaz became thoughtful and said, 'I am fearful that Lawrence will have her killed.'

'He's very cruel and merciless,' replied Mustapha Khan, 'he really could do something like that.'

'I have sworn to protect her and promised that Lawrence will not be able to cause her any harm.'

Mustapha Khan replied, 'Yes, but it would not be wise to take her out of the Residency at the moment. Lawrence would find out and immediately start action against the city.'

'That's what I thought,' Riyaz said, nodding in agreement. 'Apart from this, we will also not be able to get any more information from her from the inside.'

'You're absolutely right,' said Mustapha Khan, 'it would be best if we save her from the Residency when Maulvi Sahib attacks Lucknow.'

'Will you station some men at the southern gate?'

'Yes, I will make the arrangements . . .'

Mustapha Khan left after reassuring Riyaz, who soon fell asleep. In the evening, Shiv Mangal came to see him. He said, 'I am coming after seeing Ms Harrison. She says that Lawrence knows that the enemy's Harawal troops have reached Chinhat and his spies★ have also told him that they are about 600 strong.'

Riyaz asked, 'Did she tell you anything else?'

'Yes,' replied Shiv Mangal, 'Sir Henry Lawrence has asked for reinforcements from Mandiaown and those companies will be stationed in and around the Residency and Machchi Bhawan. Lawrence will take the white

---

★ On 29 June 1857, Sir Henry Lawrence found out that the enemy's Harawal Troops had reached Chinhat and he sent Sikh riders who came back and verified this.

Maulvi Ahmadullah Shah Sahib's Harawal Troops had actually reached Chinhat on the evening of 27 June. This place is about seven miles to the east of Lucknow on the road towards Faizabad. It is an old settlement and is well populated. There is a big lake nearby and on its banks there is a Shahi Baradari. It was one of the outer hunting houses for the Shahs of Awadh.

platoon, the artillery and a company towards Chinhat in the morning.'

Shiv Mangal was in a hurry and left straightaway, only to return after dusk. Riyaz was sitting in the courtyard speaking to an Afridi Pathan from Malihabad when Mangal returned, 'Miss Baba was right on one count. The reinforcements from Mandiaown have arrived and Lawrence is preparing to leave for Chinhat.'

'Will you go back to the Residency now?' Riyaz asked Shiv Mangal.

'I will.'

'Tell Ms Harris that tomorrow she should stay near the southern gate from morning to afternoon.'

'Right,' replied Shiv Mangal, 'I'll be off then.'

Riyaz said his night prayers and fell asleep after eating. In the morning, he got up for the dawn prayers and no sooner had he finished, than Mustapha Khan arrived.

His eyes were bloodshot and drowsy. Riyaz said, 'Looks like you didn't sleep all night.'

'I haven't slept a wink since day before yesterday and I just couldn't keep my eyes open, so I had a cup of tea.'

'Have some cardamom and honey. That should get rid of the drowsiness.'

Mustapha Khan shouted to the servants to bring breakfast. Qaim Reza appeared and, handing Riyaz a piece of paper, said, 'Ms Harris has sent this for you.'

Since he could read English, he opened the letter and his eyes gleamed with delight as he scanned it. Mustapha Khan and Qaim Reza peered over his shoulder.

'Alice has sent a map of the Residency and has also given exact details of where Lawrence has stationed the guards.'

'This is invaluable,' said Mustapha Khan. 'If the firangs are surrounded and try to fight back, we will break their defences.'

Qaim Reza interjected, 'We should keep a copy of this.'

Mustapha Khan copied out the map and Riyaz translated and wrote down the details in Urdu. They finished their breakfast. Riyaz stowed the map inside his saddle, mounted his horse and set off at a canter. He got into a boat near Shah Najaf and got off on the other bank.

In Nishatganj, about fifty men armed with guns, swords, spears and other weapons were standing in front of a haveli.

As Riyaz walked past them, one of the men called out, 'Riyaz Ahmad Khan, you should leave quickly. A firangi patrol and a Sikh patrol have just passed by here. They have gone to the Residency and will return with more forces.'

Riyaz recognized the man as one of the deputies of Mirza Haider Baig. Riyaz spurred on his horse and reached Kukrail, passing Maahnagar. He passed small groups of villagers walking on the roads. They were all his army's spies. He saw another villager near Kukrail carrying a *lathi* with a small brass *lutia* and a piece of string attached to it. Riyaz smiled as the man was none other than his old friend Jawahar Singh.

Jawahar Singh greeted him from afar, approached him and said, 'Riyaz Bhaiyya, go quickly. Maulvi Sahib is waiting for you. A Sikh patrol and firangi spies just passed through here and I told them that there are 200 or 250

men* waiting in an orchard. The others also told them the same thing.'

The sun was setting and Riyaz's horse broke into a gallop. He soon reached Ismailganj.† Maulvi Ahmadullah Shah Sahib was pacing around an orchard along with Subedar Ghamandi‡ Singh. Riyaz got off his horse, handed Maulvi Sahib Alice's map and, apprising him of the situation, set off again for the city.

---

* The English had been informed by their spies that there were only 600 or so men in the area.
† Ismailganj is a village near Kukrail between Chinhat and Lucknow. This is where Lawrence was defeated and from where he fled back to the Residency.
‡ Ghamandi Singh was a subedar in the army and when he found out that the War Council had crowned Prince Birjees Qadr king, he got upset and removed his troops from the Residency. However, later he took part again in the siege. (Qaiser-al-tawarikh).

11

The Battle of Ismailganj

The reinforcements from Mandiaown had reached the Residency and Machchi Bhawan by dusk and had been stationed at various places. The English had prepared to fight under siege. By the first week of June, Sir Henry Lawrence knew that there was no way to leave Lucknow and had thus reinforced the defences of the Residency. Major Anderson and Captain Fulton had doubled the guard and created strong defences. Sir Henry spent the night of 29 June consulting his officers and, on the morning of 30 June,* along with the English platoon, the Sikh regiment, cannon, artillery and native sepoys, he left for Chinhat.

Apart from native and English artillery, the forces also had eight-inch trench cannons, being pulled by elephants. On the way, Lawrence asked some villagers about the

---

* On 30 June, the Hindustani army fought against the Company forces in Ismailganj.

strength of the other army. One of them said, 'Sir, I saw about fifty or sixty armed cavalrymen.'

Further on, near Maahnagar, another villager informed him that a reconnaissance patrol of the Hindustani army had passed by earlier but then had gone back. The English were certain of their superiority, thinking that they would defeat the Hindustani army within two hours and return to the Residency for lunch. The information given by the villagers buoyed their spirits as they continued towards Chinhat.

Sir Henry Lawrence, Lieutenant Colonel Inglis and Colonel Palmer thought the Hindustani army would turn heel and run when they heard the English forces coming. They were wrong. As soon as they reached Ismailganj, they were surrounded and fire rained on them from all sides. Fighting for the freedom of their homeland, the forces of the Hindustani army led by Maulvi Ahmadullah Shah had reached Ismailganj and hidden in the mango orchards on both sides of the road that went towards Faizabad. The Hindustani army had stationed itself near the village of Ismailganj with loaded cannons and was waiting to let loose on the English army.

The fire from the Hindustani cannons and the assault by the soldiers caused mayhem among the English. The Hindustani artillery officers used their swords to cut the ropes that tied the cannons to the horses and pushed the cannons into a ditch. The Sikh infantrymen were also engulfed and ran in whichever direction they were facing.

The sounds of the cannons being fired and the ordnance exploding disturbed the elephants that were dragging the eight-inch guns. In their excitement, they ran towards the Hindustani army. A few whites and some native sepoys tried to stop them but they were crushed by the stampede.

Lawrence's army was surrounded on all sides and his men were falling like pins. There was nowhere to run and Lawrence was riding from one side to the other with his cap in his hand, cursing himself for bringing his army into this hellhole.

Some of the English officers were trying to offer enticements to the Sikh and native sepoys to stay and fight, to no avail. Meanwhile, the Hindustani cannons were firing away and the Hindustani army was tearing through clouds of smoke and hurtling towards Lawrence's forces.

Under the relentless cannon fire, Lawrence ordered his forces to retreat and they fled, leaving behind their equipment and weapons. Maulvi Ahmadullah Shah was standing in an orchard and watching the fighting through a telescope. Seeing Lawrence's forces fleeing, Maulvi Ahmadullah Shah gave orders to the infantries of Mahmudabad and Ramnagar Dhamedi to pursue them. They chased the English army into the city and arrived there the next morning at 10 o'clock.

As news of Lawrence's defeat spread in Lucknow, there was absolute pandemonium. People came out into the streets to swear fealty to the Hindustani army and took up arms to throw out the English from their homeland. To keep the peace, Mustapha Khan and Mirza Haider Baig had stationed men throughout the city. When Riyaz entered the city, he saw more than 500 armed men from Qaiserbagh going towards the river, led by Mustapha Khan's deputy, Thakur

Tribeni Singh. Riyaz called out to him to stop, approached him and said, 'Thakur, don't go towards the river yet.'

'But the fighting has started, and if we attack the Residency right now, we will be able to capture it,' replied the Thakur.

'Lawrence has placed cannons everywhere,' countered Riyaz, 'all of you just have rifles. Maulvi Sahib will enter the city shortly and he has six artillery batteries. It will be better to fight cannons with cannons.'

The thunder of the cannons from Ismailganj could be heard in Lucknow. Thakur Tribeni Singh left for Taare Wali Kothi. Riyaz set off towards the house of Mustapha Khan, bumping into his old companions Jawahar Singh, Laxman Pandey and Ramzan Khan. They were leading 600 armed men towards the Residency. The column of men was mostly made up of Riyaz's platoon. Riyaz asked Jawahar Singh, 'Where are you going?'

'To attack the Residency,' Jawahar Singh replied, 'Lawrence and Brigadier Ingles are not there and we can easily take it and fly our flag from its ramparts.'

'No,' Riyaz said emphatically, 'Maulvi Sahib is on his way and Lawrence won't be able to hold out there much longer.'

Laxman Pandey looked towards the sky, deduced the distance of the army from Lucknow from the echo of cannon fire, and said, 'Maulvi Sahib is on the move.'

Ramzan Khan nodded vigorously in agreement, 'Yes, the sounds are getting closer.'

Riyaz said, 'Go towards the Residency, disperse quietly into the alleys and lanes and wait there.'

'Where are you going?' asked Jawahar Singh.

'Towards the southern gate of the Residency,' replied Riyaz. 'Ms Alice Harrison will be waiting for me there and I need to get more information from her.'

'Right! We will also head in that direction.'

When Riyaz reached Enayat Bagh, he divided the men into groups of 100 and stationed them at various roundabouts and alleys. Ramzan Khan interjected, 'Some riflemen just passed by but they have defected and joined Mustapha Khan's forces.'

'They had promised that many of them would cross over,' replied Riyaz. 'I'm sure some of them have also joined Raja Jai Lal Singh's forces.'

Two cavalrymen came galloping from the direction of Qaiserbagh and, breathing heavily, said, 'Lawrence's men are headed this way.'

'By which road?' asked Riyaz.

'They'll go past the bridge of boats to the Residency.'

The other horseman spoke, 'If we attack them from this side, they will definitely lay down their arms.'

Jawahar Singh, Laxman Pandey and Ramzan Khan took 300 men and double-marched towards Tehri Kothi. Riyaz took 100 men, reached the southern gate of the Residency and stood where the single-floor houses were, opposite the gate.

Lawrence had reached the banks of the Gomti. Jawahar Singh and his men levelled their rifles at the oncoming force but, just before firing, stopped. The Hindustani army was in such hot pursuit that they too would have been hit by the volley of fire. Jawahar called out to his men to wait, went round and positioned himself near Tehri Kothi.

Lawrence's forces were in a state of complete disarray. Some were walking two by two, others were on horseback, yet others were sitting astride cannons and, in the last rows, men were trying to help the wounded.* Jawahar Singh thought of firing on them from the cover of the ditch but realized that the cannon fire from the Residency walls was targeting his brothers-in-arms. He decided to move along the ditch towards Enayat Bagh, while the men from the Hindustani army, guns ablaze and cannons in tow, rushed towards the Residency and started fanning out, surrounding it on all sides.

This was the moment Riyaz was waiting for. Lawrence and his men had not even had a chance to breathe when Riyaz attacked the southern gate. Fifty native sepoys came out of the gate and as soon as the whiteys saw them leaving, they rained a volley of fire on them. Riyaz's companions hurtled towards the southern gate, shouting slogans, urging on their forces.

Riyaz saw a few whiteys outside the residence of John Harrison and fired. A few of them fell straight away while others clambered over a wall and fled. Alice was standing in the veranda behind a pillar and waved her handkerchief. Riyaz shouted for her and she screamed and ran towards the gate. Someone fired at Alice from a rooftop and the bullet whistled past her ear. She dived into a flower bed and started crawling. Riyaz fired back in the direction of the shot and looked towards Alice.

She screamed, 'Stay there! I'm coming!'

---

* *The Siege of Lucknow* by Lady Inglis.

Another shot rang out from the rooftop and a man standing next to Riyaz collapsed with a thud. Another man caught him and, propping him up, ran towards the gate. Riyaz and his men started firing at the roof without stopping. Alice had crawled her way towards Riyaz. He caught hold of her hand and ran towards the gate while the other men continued to fire towards the roof. As soon as he was outside, he called out to his men and they fled into an alley. Riyaz was still holding Alice's hand and she was pulling him towards herself. Just then some cannons from the Hindustani army arrived and started firing at the Residency.

Alice turned to Riyaz, pulling him, and said, 'Riyaz, don't stay here. They have placed the nine-pound cannon facing this direction. It will reduce these houses to rubble.'

There was a rumble and a thunderclap from inside the Residency and the walls of one of the houses were smashed to bits. The artillerymen took the cannons to a safe distance and started pounding the Residency. The cracks of rifle shots and the sound of cannon firing filled the air. Riyaz lifted Alice, putting her on a horse and, mounting his own, they rushed towards Mustapha Khan's haveli. There were fifty or sixty men standing near the gate who saluted as Riyaz rode past them.

Riyaz went inside and made Alice sit in a room while he called one of the servants and said, 'Look, Miss Baba is going to stay here for the time being. Make sure she is comfortable and that no harm befalls her.'

'Whatever you command, sir,' replied the servant. 'Don't worry, I will stay here myself.'

'You haven't understood,' said Riyaz. 'You do not need to guard her, but protect her. She is one of us!'

'Ah, well, she will not have any kind of problem, I assure you.'

Riyaz went to another room, changed into his uniform and came back to see Alice.

'Please don't mind, Ms Alice, but I cannot keep you company.'

'Quite right. This is not the time to sit around. Your brothers-in-arms have thrown themselves into the fight for the freedom of their homeland and you too should go and do your duty. Lawrence has decided to lock down the Residency and fight the siege until the end,' replied Alice.

'Lawrence has decided this but he can also change his mind. One never knows what can happen in a battle,' Riyaz countered.

'Please don't mind my speaking so informally, Riyaz.'

'This kind of talk is . . .' replied Riyaz with a smile. 'I shall leave now, with your permission.'

'Yes, of course. God speed.'

Riyaz left the house and rode towards Qaiserbagh. Near Malika Zamania's Imamabada, he bumped into Mirza Haider Baig who authoritatively said, 'The Hindustani forces laid siege to the Residency at precisely 11 o'clock and now it is being shelled from all sides.'

'Where is Maulvi Sahib?' asked Riyaz.

'He's gone towards Taare Wali Kothi and Raja Jai Lal Singh has also gone in that direction.'

Riyaz spurred his horse on and saw Subedar Ghamandi Singh. He dismounted, had a brief chat with him and continued riding towards Taare Wali Kothi.

Outside the kothi, there were about 2000 Hindustani soldiers and Maulvi Sahib was pacing before them, explaining something. Riyaz got off his horse outside the gate and waited. Maulvi Sahib dismissed the soldiers and motioned to Riyaz. He asked him, 'Do you have any new information?'

'No, but I managed to get the English girl out of the Residency,' replied Riyaz. 'She was in great danger there. I think Lawrence would have found some excuse to have her killed.'

'He will get killed himself,' Maulvi Sahib replied as he gazed towards the sky. 'He is very powerful. Go and ask Ms Alice Harrison which room he tends to sit in and come back here in two hours. I shall be waiting.'

Riyaz went to Mustapha Khan's house. Alice was sleeping in a reclining armchair. She heard footsteps, woke up and sat upright. Riyaz went towards her, pulled up a chair and said, 'Which room does Lawrence sit in?'

'I sent you two maps of the Residency. Do you have either one with you?'

'I have one,' replied Riyaz as he took the map out of his pocket. 'The Residency is being shelled as we speak and if it continues like this, then we will be able to enter by nightfall.'

'No,' countered Alice, 'you still don't know the strength of the Residency's defences.'

'You might be right,' he replied as he handed her the map, 'but our will is stronger.'

Alice looked at the map and, pointing to one spot, said, 'This is the room.'

'If we start shelling it from the side of Tehri Kothi, we can reduce it to rubble.'

'You shouldn't delay any further,' Alice said with urgency. 'The magazine and arsenal are still in Machchi Bhawan.'

'I will go and inform Maulvi Sahib straightaway that we need to capture Machchi Bhawan and . . .'

Alice interjected, 'If you don't capture Machchi Bhawan today, Lawrence will blow it up.'

Riyaz looked at Alice, thinking. His brow furrowed. Seeing him worrying, Alice said, 'Don't worry. Your cause is righteous, and God is with you.'

'Are you sure that he will blow up the magazine today?' asked Riyaz.

'This is what he has decided. Last night, he said that if the Hindustani army captures the Residency, he will blow up the magazine in Machchi Bhawan.'

'Anything else?' asked Riyaz.

'Lawrence has told the troops stationed in the Residency that if they protect and hold it, he will make them rich beyond their dreams.'

'And . . .?'

'Oh, and this morning he sent twenty men to Allahabad and another twenty to Kanpur.'

Riyaz stood up. As he was about to leave, Alice said, 'Food is ready. The servant just informed me. Why don't you eat? Who knows when you will get a chance.'

'Have you eaten?'

'No,' replied Alice, 'I thought I would eat with you when you came back.'

Riyaz called out to the servant to lay the *dastarkhan* and ate with Alice. After about half an hour, he left.

The Hindustani armies were still attacking ferociously and the cannons of the Residency were still thundering away. Riyaz went to find Maulvi Ahmadullah Shah but he had not returned, so Riyaz paced up and down near the gate. In the late afternoon, he offered his prayers. Maulvi Sahib returned by eight in the evening and Riyaz told him all that he had learnt.

'Raja Jai Lal Singh has gone towards the Residency, and if, for some reason, he does not attack by nightfall, then later at night Mir Muhtasham Bilgrami will attack Machchi Bhawan and take it over.'

Riyaz spoke to Maulvi Sahib about a few other logistical matters and took his leave.

12

The Crowning of Birjees Qadr

The next evening, Riyaz and a few of his colleagues gathered at the house of Mustapha Khan. Riyaz addressed Mustapha Khan, saying, 'Khan Sahib, Ms Alice Harrison is under our protection. She has told us of Lawrence's secret plans which will help us secure a victory, Insha Allah. Her well-being and comfort is incumbent upon us.'

'Of course, she is one of us,' replied Mustapha Khan, 'but I'm afraid we are all busy and there are no other women in the house, so the best thing would be to take her to Mir Sahib's house.'

Ms Alice was listening to their conversation from the other room. As soon as Mustapha Khan had finished speaking, she came into the room and addressed Riyaz, 'If my presence here is not disrupting your work, let me stay here. I want to help these brave men who are fighting for the freedom of their homeland.'

'How, Miss Baba, will you be of help to them?' Jawahar Singh asked Alice.

'I can treat the wounded.'

Mustapha Khan interjected, 'In that case, you will have to stay in one of the buildings in Qaiserbagh which has been temporarily converted into a hospital by Maulvi Sahib.'

'I am ready to go there,' replied Alice.

'Right, I shall go to Maulvi Sahib and inform him of your decision.'

'Wait, I don't think this is the best option,' interjected Riyaz. 'Right now, every Hindustani is baying for the blood of the English and she looks like one. Someone, overcome with thoughts of revenge, might harm her. It would be better if she was taken to a safer place.'

'Riyaz, why are you opposing this plan?' Alice exclaimed.

'For your safety. You don't know how bad the situation is, otherwise you wouldn't have volunteered to treat the wounded.'

'You're right,' said Ramzan Khan, 'the situation is bad and it isn't the right time for her to go and tend the wounded.'

The relentless sound of cannons unleashing volley after volley came from the direction of the Residency.

Jawahar Singh spoke up, 'We should be on our way now. We can decide this tomorrow.'

'The wives of two of my servants have just arrived,' Mustapha Khan said. 'They shall look after her.'

'Please don't neglect your duties on my account. Anyway, we can resolve this matter tomorrow. If you do not want me to stay here, then perhaps you can have me escorted to Kanpur.'

'Please make yourself at home,' replied Mustapha Khan. 'It is no trouble at all and I assure you, no harm will come to you. You have walked away from your own people and helped us with invaluable information. There is no way we will send you away.'

Alice left to go into the other room. Mustapha Khan faced Riyaz, 'Riyaz Sahib, the armies from your area are attacking the Residency next to the river. Why don't you head in that direction and see if they need any supplies?'

'Yes, Riyaz Bhaiyya,' exclaimed Jawahar Singh, 'I too am going in that direction because Subedar Sahib said that he wants some of us to look after the food and supplies and make sure nothing is lacking.'

They briskly walked out of the house talking to each other and, as Riyaz mounted his horse, he turned to Ramzan Khan, 'Ramzan Khan Sahib, meet Maulvi Sahib and see if he has a message for me. I am going towards the river with Jawahar Singh. If Machchi Bhawan is captured at night, we will shell the Residency from there.'

Jawahar Singh also mounted his horse and they set off towards the river. Jawahar Singh said, 'Riyaz Bhaiyya, I don't think keeping Ms Alice here is wise under any circumstances. Others don't know the background and will think that we have spirited her away from the Residency because she is young and beautiful.'

'Thakur, this is exactly what I feel,' replied Riyaz.

'Why not send her to Mankapur? Ram Tirath Pandey will look after her well. As we speak, there are four firangi men, five women and eight or ten children in his haveli. I heard that the commander of the other army's military police asked for them to be handed over but he refused.'

'Pandey Ji is a very kind man,' Riyaz said thoughtfully. 'Alice definitely won't face any problems there.'

'Bhaiyya, in my opinion, have her sent there.'

'Hmm, we'll see tomorrow,' replied Riyaz, spurring on his horse. 'I don't even know when the Residency will fall.'

'Until that old bastard is alive, we won't be able to take it.'

'Are you speaking about Lawrence?'

'Yes,' replied Jawahar Singh, 'because of that wretch, this war is getting prolonged. He is very stubborn and, by God, he hates us Indians.'

'The armies that are coming from Faizabad have started looting the city.'

'Raja Jai Lal Singh has gone to speak to the officers in Nusratganj. They are all in the Taare Wali Kothi.'

They soon reached the riverside, right behind where their troops were fighting. The artillery was belching out cannonballs. The fighting continued all night and the next morning. Raja Jai Lal Singh called the kotwal, Reza Ali Baig, and said, 'There is open looting and arson in the city. You need to control this.'

'Janaab-e-Aali, what can I can do?' asked Reza Ali Baig. 'The riflemen have run away and it is not possible for our armies to control the mobs.'

'The Akhtari and Naderi platoons* have merged with the Hindustani armies and are attacking the Residency.'

---

* Akhtari and Naderi were famous platoons in Wajid Ali Shah's army that the British disbanded.

Raja Jai Lal Singh replied, 'The officers have told their soldiers that they must not loot. I am sure they won't anymore.'

'Raja Sahib,' replied Reza Ali Baig, 'until a leader does not emerge, peace will not be possible. It would be wise to crown someone and let the forces fight in his name.'

'This is what we were discussing in the Taare Wali Kothi last night,' said Raja Jai Lal Singh. 'But Ruknaddaula Nawab Mohammad Hasan Khan has already been arrested and imprisoned in the Residency by the British. That leaves Prince Birjees Qadr.'

'If you think it is appropriate, why don't you crown Sultan-e-Alam's* stepbrother, Dara Sitwat Mirza Mohammad Reza Khan?'

Raja Jai Lal Singh replied, 'He is weak-headed!'

They both continued to speak and, when they could not figure out what to do, Raja Jai Lal Singh said, 'We can discuss this at the Majlis-e Shura† tomorrow.'

'Whatever you think is best,' replied Reza Ali Baig. 'But remember that the firangis will not be easily defeated. Last night they blew up Machchi Bhawan‡. They could shell Qaiserbagh and other buildings.'

---

* This was one of the titles of Wajid Ali Shah.

† A consultative meeting where consensus is taken from the participants. Somewhat akin to a modern parliament.

‡ After the siege of the Residency, Sir Henry Lawrence decided to withdraw from Machchi Bhawan and gave the order to Garrison Engineer Captain Fulton to withdraw all the companies stationed there at exactly midnight. The order to blow up Machchi Bhawan was issued to Lieutenant Thomas who carried it out as soon as Machchi Bhawan was cleared.

Maulvi Ahmadullah Shah had temporarily stationed men throughout the city in order to maintain peace while he went to the various artillery units to inspect the cannons and encourage the men to fight on. He carried with him the map of the Residency that Alice had given Riyaz.

The next morning, he called the famous gun sergeant Kale Khan who was posted near Tehri Kothi and, showing him the map, said, 'Kale Khan, the vicious man who is responsible for Hindustanis slaughtering Hindustanis is in this room.' He pointed to the map. 'Tell me, where do you think it is from here?'

Kale Khan worked out where the building was, and looking towards the Residency, said, 'Sir, I sent a cannonball through the roof of that very room yesterday.'

'But that tyrant is still alive.'

Kale Khan was a very formidable figure. He immediately went towards one of the cannons and changed its direction. He then took out a watch from the pocket of his Turkish coat and motioned towards one of his colleagues.

The man loaded a cannonball into the mouth of the cannon and waited for further orders. Kale Khan kept his eye on his watch and, when the needles reached nine o'clock, he gave the signal. The gunner lit the fuse and there was a loud explosion followed by smoke as the cannonball found its target.* Maulvi Ahmadullah Shah hugged Kale Khan.

---

* At precisely nine o'clock on 2 July 1857, a cannonball hit a room in the north-eastern corner of the Residency and ripped Sir Henry Lawrence's left leg off from the thigh. The previous day, another cannonball had hit the room but both Sir Henry Lawrence and his secretary George Cooper escaped harm by the skin of their teeth. The British officers had advised

That very evening, the Majlis-e Shura decided to coronate Prince Birjees Qadr, but the conditions and formalities were discussed for almost three days. On 5 July 1857, which was the 12th of Ziq'ad 1273 Hijri, the crown was placed on Birjees Qadr's head by Shahabuddeen and Risaldar Syed Barkat Ahmad in the presence of various officers. As they congratulated the new king, the cannons fired a gun salute but they used real cannonballs and sent them flying towards the Residency.

Meanwhile, the various officeholders and ministers of the court were notified and mobilized. Most of the army was in favour of Birjees Qadr but a number of people from Lucknow who were sympathetic to the poor subjects were opposed to it.

Riyaz made his way to Mustapha Khan's house.

'So Riyaz Sahib, did you see the injustice of the army officers?'

'Yes, Khan Sahib, I too was not in favour of the coronation of Prince Birjees Qadr and Subedar Ghamandi Singh is very angry. He plans to remove his forces from the Bailey Guard tomorrow morning.'

'I don't think this should happen yet. We need to defeat the enemy, then we can decide what is to be done.'

'I am leaving for Mahmudabad in the morning.'

'Has Raja Sahib called for you?'

'No. I have to take a letter from Maulvi Sahib.'

Lawrence after the first hit that he should change rooms but Lawrence insisted that no Indian would hit the same target twice. Lawrence died thirty-six hours after his leg was blown off, on 4 July 1857.

'A contingent of Pasis has arrived from Mahmudabad this morning and brought lots of supplies.'

'Our Raja Sahib won't rest until he has thrown the firangis out of our country. He will sacrifice everything.'

Mustapha Khan paused and replied, 'Those who sacrifice everything for their fellow man are blessed with immortality.'

Alice walked into the room and said, 'Riyaz, please take me to Mahmudabad as well.'

'Fine, I shall take you with me tomorrow. Will you be able to ride for five to ten kilometres on a horse?'

'Yes,' replied Alice, 'all the women in the Residency at the moment are great riders.'

Mirza Haider Baig and Ramzan Khan also arrived. They ate together, then Mirza Haider Baig and Ramzan Khan left. Riyaz was exhausted so he went to sleep after offering his night prayers.

In the morning he set off for Mahmudabad with Alice. Twenty armed men accompanied them. On the way, Riyaz turned to Alice and said, 'I will drop you at Mankapur. You will be well looked after by Pandey Ji and there are a number of firangi men and women there.'

'Whatever you want. What can I say?'

'I trust Pandey Ji,' replied Riyaz. 'He is true to his word and will do what he promises.'

They reached Mankapur at eleven that morning. Ram Tirath welcomed them warmly. Riyaz handed over Alice and got to the point, saying, 'Pandey Ji, you have to protect her with your life if necessary. I am leaving her in your care.'

'Riyaz, my son, you don't need to say anything more. She will be a guest of my daughter and I swear that as long as I am alive, no one will be able to so much as look in her direction.'

They sat together and talked until lunch, after which Riyaz got ready to leave.

Alice quietly said, 'I will wait for you here, Riyaz. Don't forget about me.'

'How can you say that?' Riyaz told her reassuringly. 'There is no way that I can forget you.'

He left Mankapur and arrived in Mahmudabad after sunset. Raja Nawab Ali Khan had scouts in place all the way from Mahmudabad to Lucknow and he was getting regular news and updates. He read Maulvi Sahib's letter and wrote a reply. He called Riyaz and said, 'Riyaz, even though it seems like we have an advantage, I am afraid the signs are not good.'

'Sarkar*, I don't understand what you mean.'

The arrogance and over-confidence of our officers will harm our cause and all our hard work will go to nothing.'

'Personally, if you permit me to say, I do not feel like there is any such problem.'

'You are a young man,' replied Raja Sahib. 'Maulvi Sahib also shares similar views which he has written in this letter to me. Anyway, we have to do our duty. Defeat and victory are ultimately in God's hands. Go home and rest and meet me in the morning before you leave for Lucknow.'

---

* Translator's note: *Sarkar* literally means government, but the term is also often used to address people of high rank.

Riyaz stayed with his parents and left for Lucknow in the morning, carrying Raja Sahib's letter. He briefly stopped in Mankapur to meet Alice and Pandey Ji and then carried on to Lucknow.

The Hindustani forces were still shelling the Residency but in turn the Residency's defences were unrelenting. When he reached Lucknow, he heard from Mustapha Khan and Jawahar Singh that reinforcements were regularly coming into Lucknow but the problem was that each commanding officer seemed to be primarily concerned with his own power. They were not interested in those who had been involved in the uprising since the beginning; neither did they accept their leadership.

Riyaz went to see Maulvi Ahmadullah Shah. He carefully read and reread the letter, folded it and put it away in his pocket. He paced around his room. Seeing the palpable worry on Maulvi Sahib's face, Riyaz said, 'You are the leader of the uprising and everyone has chosen you and sworn an oath to follow your commands. Pass orders and if someone disobeys, we will take disciplinary action against that person.'

'Riyaz Ahmad Khan! Ultimately, God wills what happens. I have to do my duty and if God wills it, the flag of Bahadur Shah Zafar will stay aloft.'

'Sarkar is also not happy with the behaviour of the officers,' replied Riyaz.

'That is what he has written to me, but he will remain steadfast to our cause until the end. I too will not back down.'

After a while, Riyaz returned to his camp on the other bank of the Gomti River. One of the subedars of his forces had been hurt in the shelling but was relentlessly fighting on. The next day, Riyaz also joined the fighting. He tried to use the ditch in order to access the Residency but the British had put cannons there. He got ready again on the third day to fight on the frontlines but the subedar stopped him, 'Riyaz, take twenty riders and head towards Purwa. The Raja of Rai Bareilly, Beni Madhao, has pitched camp there and stationed troops all the way to Mangal Dara so that the British cannot get reinforcements from Kanpur. He has a lot of gunpowder, so bring back as much as you can.'

Riyaz left with twenty horsemen and returned on 14 July. By then, the army had shelled their way through many of the Residency walls but the British defended these breaches by placing cannons there. The Hindustani army's soldiers were unable to get into the Residency.

Raja Loni Singh's reinforcements had arrived. They began to prepare to attack the Residency but their officers were unfamiliar with its layout.

Maulvi Sahib made Riyaz head of a unit of 500 of his soldiers. On the morning of 20 July, Riyaz began to rain fire on one side and attack the Residency from the other. He was able to reach the walls and twenty of his men entered the Residency through a break. He was planning to hide inside as well when suddenly there was a large boom outside the wall and a tunnel blew up and collapsed.

Everything was covered in a cloud of dust and smoke. The English took advantage of this and redirected their cannon fire towards Riyaz's men. Faced with direct fire, Riyaz's forces scattered helter-skelter and the men at the back retreated. Riyaz tried to enter the Residency with some of his men from another side but they faced unrelenting fire. Eventually, they too were forced to retreat though they managed to kill eight to ten whities. They reached their encampment by two in the afternoon.

13

The Struggle

Despite the internal differences within the Hindustani army, the siege of the Residency continued. The reinforcements that came from Nizamat-e-Khairabad* mostly comprised men from Raja Nawab Ali Khan and Raja Loni Singh's armies. Raja Nawab Ali Khan toured his area raising troops, sending fresh supplies and cooks and having canteens set up in the outlying areas of Lucknow where soldiers could get hot meals.

Raja Nawab Ali Khan had also promised the officers that if, for some reason, the salaries of the soldiers could not be paid by the king's court in Awadh, he would make the

---

* Awadh was divided into four divisions: Nizamat-e-Bahraich, Nizamat-e-Faizabad, Nizamat-e-Khairabad, and Nizamat-e-Lucknow. The nizamat was also referred to as a division and each division had its own commissioner. Each division was further divided into a number of districts and each of these had a deputy commissioner. The chief commissioner was based in Lucknow.

payments himself. The only condition was that the soldiers should not retreat from the territory they had gained. On 6 August, Riyaz met Raja Sahib in Sidhauli where he had camped in a large field and was ordering troops to march towards Lucknow. Regular reinforcements were being sent by the Thakur chiefs of Mithauli, Ramnagar Dhamedi,⋆ Dhaurara and other places. Raja Nawab Ali Khan had made arrangements for a large encampment where the soldiers would be welcomed and given all the necessary information. After a short stay of two days and the necessary debrief, the men would form into companies and march to Lucknow. In case their arms were not up to the mark or if they didn't have arms, the Mahmudabad officers would provide them the necessary weapons. Raja Nawab Ali Khan's men had fanned out to find civil supplies and procure arms. Whenever they found the necessary items, they would send them to the central camp from where they were further sent to Lucknow.

Riyaz met Raja Sahib at the camp headquarters and, after asking him about the battlefront, Raja Sahib said, 'Riyaz, we have made all the necessary arrangements and are doing our best to keep supplies and morale high. I know that Prince Birjees Qadr's coronation is just symbolic. What can an eleven-year-old do? Especially when the capital is gripped by such fierce fighting! Mammoo Khan is powerless

---

⋆ Translator's note: The Muslim Rajas of Mahmudabad and the Hindu Rajas of Ramnagar Dhamedi were blood brothers, sworn to protect each other. For many generations when there was a wedding or festivity, elephants and other things would be sent from one to the other.

and was only included in the fifth cavalry regiment because of Begum Hazrat Mahal.'

'Yes, *huzoor*, but Sharafuddaula Mohammad Ibrahim Khan* is a very wise man.'

'I know, but I also know that he won't take an interest in anything now. He accepted the position of vazir only because of his fear of the War Council.'

Riyaz shuffled nervously.

'This leaves Hussamuddaula Daraogha† but I do not trust these people. They are all opportunists,' said Raja Sahib.

Riyaz looked towards his feet and sadness crept over his face. Noticing this, Raja Sahib said, 'Riyaz, you needn't worry. Even though I know the rot in the court in Lucknow, I will remain true to my word until my last breath.'

Riyaz asked, 'But isn't the truth with us? Won't that guarantee our victory? Will all our sacrifices be in vain?'

'No!' Raja Sahib replied emphatically. 'No one's sacrifice will be in vain. Allah always blesses and rewards those whose intentions are pure. He has said in the Quran,

---

* Sharafuddaula Mohammad Ibrahim Khan was one of Lucknow's most accomplished and wise politicians. He was a vazir in the court of Wajid Ali Shah but was forcefully removed because Wajid Ali Shah was angry with him. He also tried to exile him but was unsuccessful. The resident general of Lucknow had deep respect for him. After the siege of the Residency and the coronation of Birjees Qadr, Sharafuddaula was appointed vazir again by the War Council.

† Hussamuddaula was Wajid Ali Shah's uncle. After Wajid Ali Shah's exile, he was made responsible for looking after the king's properties and eventually the War Council made him Chief of Security.

"But they do not believe that they will be rewarded." Our hard work will not go to waste. This is my firm belief.'

'Then, huzoor, what are my orders?'

'Give the soldiers this message from me . . .'

Riyaz kissed Raja Sahib's hands and stood up.

'Riyaz, your father will return from Mankapur this week. Ram Tirath Pandey went to call him.'

Riyaz bowed to salaam Raja Sahib and left immediately. He saw Ram Tirath Pandey in an orchard near Mankapur. After exchanging the usual greetings, he said, 'Riyaz Mian, you'll have a long life. I could be granted whatever I wished for just now.'

'Yes, Pandey Ji, I came because you thought of me. I would have gone directly to Lucknow after meeting Raja Sahib but as I was leaving he said that you had come back to Mahmudabad.'

'What could I have done except gone to Mahmudabad? Alice has been so sad ever since you left, and despite my reassurances and your sister Kaushilya's, she just keeps worrying about you. One day, I told her about your parents and she wanted me to take her to Mahmudabad immediately. But you know that Lawrence has sent dozens of Mahmudabad's finest young men to the gallows, so I knew that they would be baying for a foreigner's blood.'

'Yes,' replied Riyaz, 'my neighbour in Mahmudabad is Thakur Suraj Pal Singh. His son and some of his companions saved some Englishwomen and their children from some Thakurs near Mithauli, but when they escorted them to Lucknow, Lawrence hanged them instead of thanking them.'

'Yes Bhaiyya, this is why I didn't take her there, and when I came back I told her, on your behalf, that you would return in a few days.'

'Pandey Ji,' Riyaz asked hesitantly, 'what did you ask Abba Mian, my father?'

Ram Tirath Pandey was a man of great honesty, unable to hide anything.

He replied, 'I told him that Riyaz has left a foreign girl in my custody. She is very concerned about his safety and wants to come here.'

'B . . . but Pandey Ji,' stammered Riyaz, 'you have done something catastrophic.'

'Why?' Pandey asked, surprised. 'Why, what happened?'

'Abba Mian will think that I have kidnapped Ms Alice Harrison amidst all this confusion and have hidden her with you!'

'Bhaiyya, say Ram Ram,' Pandey Ji said softly. 'Your father knows you well, as do I, and I have told him how she offered invaluable help to the *deshbhakts* in providing information against the angrez.'

'Anyway,' replied Riyaz, 'it's good you told him everything but it would have been better if he didn't know.'

'Beta,' Pandey Ji said lovingly, 'matters like this do not stay hidden for long. Your father would have questioned my friendship and asked me why even I didn't say anything to him.'

Riyaz bowed his head, lost in his thoughts.

Pandey Ji spoke again, 'Don't worry son, I told Khan Sahib that he should make her his daughter as soon as possible. Not everyone is so lucky to find a girl as beautiful as she.'

Riyaz lifted his head and his jaw dropped.

Without paying the slightest attention to this, Pandey Ji continued, 'I am telling you not to worry. Everything will be all right. If someone sacrifices everything for you, then you are also duty bound to them.'

Riyaz stared at a tree in the distance.

Pandey Ji continued, 'Come home, eat something and then you can leave for Lucknow.'

'No, Pandey Ji,' replied Riyaz, 'I will leave directly from here.'

'Waah! How can this be? The poor soul waits for you morning and evening and you won't even go to see her?'

'Pandey Ji, my duty is more important.'

'This is what your father also used to say,' countered Pandey Ji who knew Riyaz's father very well. 'But beta, you will have to come with me. You cannot mistreat someone who sacrificed everything for you.'

'Pandey Ji, I want to reassure you that my intention in bringing Ms Alice Harrison here was not that I . . . I . . .'

'Fine, fine, I believe you but you will have to come with me.'

Riyaz gave into Pandey Ji's wishes and accompanied him to his home. Alice was sitting inside the haveli with Pandey Ji's daughter Kaushilya. As soon as she heard that Riyaz had arrived, she rushed outside and, with a broad smile, said, 'Riyaz, you came! I was just telling Kaushilya *Didi* that you would certainly come today.'

Riyaz's heart skipped a beat and he tried desperately to find the appropriate words to reply to her when Pandey Ji looked at him, smiled and said, 'Why don't you two sit inside and talk and I will have some food sent for you.'

'Come, sit,' Alice said to him excitedly, grabbing his arm and making him sit next to her on the charpoy.

'Riyaz, I am so happy here. Pandey Ji treats me like his own daughter and what makes me happier is that your parents will be here in a day or two. I will be even happier to spend time with them.'

'Yes, Pandey Ji just told me that they are coming.'

Alice asked Riyaz about the situation in Lucknow.

Riyaz replied, 'Lawrence is finished. Lieutenant–Colonel Inglis is left.'

'If the siege continues for much longer, the situation will change,' Alice observed. 'The English always take advantage of a battle that is dragging on to wear out their opponents.'

Alice Harrison was speaking in a manner in which any other angrez might not have.

'Alice, your views and way of thinking are very different from the other angrez.'

'That's because I am no longer English,' Alice countered.

'Do people really change?' Riyaz wondered out loud, looking in the other direction.

'Yes,' said a voice from behind as Pandey Ji came out of another room. 'Language and comportment can change a person.'

Riyaz and Alice stood up as soon as they saw him.

'Sit! Sit! I just wanted to ask if you want to eat here or in the *attari*? Alice has still not eaten!'

'Pandey Ji, we will eat in the attari,' Alice replied.

Riyaz ate with Alice and after a while, set off for Lucknow.

That night, Maulvi Ahmadullah Shah called Riyaz to the banks of the river and, pointing in the direction of the Residency, said, 'If we attack after shelling it from the side of Surajkund⋆, we might be able to breach the walls.' They both lay flat on the ground and crawled towards the Residency until they were nearly right underneath its walls.

There was firing from all sides and they sat under an abutment and peered towards the wall. They caught snatches of some drunken Englishmen grumbling to each other. Maulvi Ahmadullah Shah squeezed Riyaz's hand and motioned towards the wall. A man was quietly coming down the side with the help of a rope. They held their breath and stared at him. When the man had come down, he got down on all fours and started crawling like an animal. Maulvi Sahib and Riyaz also started crawling and eventually reached the ditches near the river. As the man reached the shade of the ditch, he stood up and looked in all four directions. Maulvi Sahib nudged Riyaz who leapt and landed in the ditch where the man was. Before the man could react, Riyaz placed the point of his *aabdaar khanjar*†

⋆ Surajkund was a lake between the Residency and the Iron Bridge. After Independence, in 1955, a housing colony called Riverbank was built there.

† Translator's note: *Aabdaar khanjar* means dagger.

on the man's chest and said in a stentorian voice, 'Don't you dare move or I'll bury this dagger deep in your chest.'

Meanwhile, Maulvi Sahib also came up and placed the barrel of his pistol on the man's left temple. He said to Riyaz, 'Disarm him!'

Riyaz took away his weapons and used his cummerbund to tie his hands. They marched him to their camp and in the light of the lanterns saw that he was a fair-skinned young man in army uniform.

'Who are you?' demanded Maulvi Sahib.

'I am a rider with the 70th cavalry.'

'Name . . .?'

'Rasool Khan! I was running away from the Residency.'

On searching him, they recovered a letter written in English. Riyaz could just about read it. He peered at it in the darkness of the night and said, 'This letter is addressed to the Raja of Balrampur, Digvijay Singh. His help has been sought.'

Maulvi Sahib immediately sent Rasool Khan to the Taare Wali Kothi.

Two days later, Riyaz attacked the Residency with 200 men and reached its walls yet again, but the walls were very high and some English artillery was placed right there. The men went into a small ditch and the Hindustani artillery began shelling the walls. Before dusk, they managed to breach a 30-foot section of the wall. Riyaz and his men stormed the Residency but the English returned fire and they had to retreat.

Cannon fire continued to rain down on the Residency from the direction of the river. Riyaz was tired, so he made his way to Mustapha Khan's house. Four days later, they tried to breach the walls again but were unable to.

Eighteen days afterwards, another huge assault was planned on the Residency under the leadership of Mir Muhtasham Bilgrami but the Hindustani artillery wasn't able to advance quickly enough and the men had to retreat despite inflicting heavy damages on the English. The morning of that attack, Riyaz had to go back to see Raja Nawab Ali Khan of Mahmudabad.

On the way, he stopped in Mankapur where his parents, brothers and sisters had already arrived. His father sprung up to embrace his courageous young son and wouldn't let him go. His mother hugged him and held him tightly as she prayed for his health and long life. Alice was also standing there with his brothers and sisters who all were beaming with pride. She was completely silent, wearing Awadhi clothes. Riyaz's sister asked him, 'Do you recognize this lady?'

Riyaz smiled nervously as small beads of perspiration appeared on his forehead. His father went into the courtyard while his mother said to Alice, 'Come here, beti, why are you standing there?'

Red in the face, Alice came and sat next to them.

'She is such a wonderful girl,' Riyaz's mother said as she placed her hands on Alice's shoulders. 'In just a few days, she has won our hearts, even though . . .'

'Ammi, please don't say this,' interrupted Alice. 'I have forsaken my people for good and if I wanted to remain with them, I wouldn't have come here . . .'

Pandey Ji called out from outside and Riyaz got up to leave. Riyaz stayed for a day and left early the next day, reaching Lucknow by the afternoon. The situation had not changed and Maulvi Sahib had spent the entire morning in consultation with his officers. Mustapha Khan told him that ammunition supplies were running out and that the reinforcements and supplies coming from Farrukhabad had been captured by a Raja who was aligned with the British. They had to attack the Raja. Maulvi Sahib told him the same thing the next morning and sent 1000 riders in that direction. Two weeks later, the forces returned with the ammunition and the Hindustani army restarted its assault.

Riyaz advised that a tunnel be dug from Surajkund to the Residency. The officers liked the advice and the first tunnel started from the ditch. Riyaz thought that this would be a good way to blow up the walls and send soldiers into the Residency. However, a spy informed Inglis about the plan and he had the tunnel collapsed before anything could be done.

Risaldar Barkat Ahmad started the second tunnel under Riyaz's supervision. No more than twenty or twenty-two yards of the tunnel had been dug than Riyaz was called again to see Raja Nawab Ali Khan. He was in charge of the tunnel and left his responsibilities to Jawahar Singh. Raja Nawab Ali Khan had just returned from touring his area. Riyaz immediately went to call on him and handed over Maulvi Ahmadullah Shah's letter.

Maulvi Ahmadullah Shah had written that the Raja of Balrampur should be pressed upon to participate in the uprising and if he refused, he should be arrested and charged with aiding and abetting the enemy. Raja Sahib called his advisers and asked them for their counsel. One of them said,

'Huzoor, he is our neighbour and the families have known each other for generations. It's better if you do not take part in this and leave it to the army officers in Lucknow.'

Riyaz had been allowed to sit in the meeting and agreed with the adviser. 'I agree. The armies will be able to capture the fort of Balrampur within a few hours but it would not be right of us to attack our neighbours. The bullets that would be used to attack them should be used to attack the angrez and force them to leave India.'

'Yes, Riyaz Mian,' replied Raja Sahib thoughtfully, 'I agree with your counsel. Bring me some paper and a pen and I shall write to Maulvi Ahmadullah Shah immediately.'

He wrote the letter hurriedly and, handing it to Riyaz, said, 'Riyaz Mian, instead of going to Lucknow directly, go through Shahjahanpur. Maulvi Sahib needs the help of some good gunsmiths to repair rifles. You will find Nabiullah Khan in Shahjahanpur. He is the best gunsmith in our entire province.'

Riyaz ate his lunch, offered his afternoon prayers and left. By nightfall, he arrived at Sitapur.

14

Bloody Warfronts

After the coronation of Birjees Qadr, the War Council had made Maharaja Bal Krishn the commander of the armies. But a short while later, the Prime Minister, Sharafuddaula Nawab Mohammad Ibrahim Khan's nephew, Muzaffar Ali Khan, was made commander on the request of Mirzai Begum. He was given charge but the officers continued to do as they pleased. In name, Muzaffar Ali Khan was the leader but the officers only paid heed to their superiors.

Maulvi Ahmadullah Shah was trying to fix the problems and Sharafuddaula Nawab Mohammad Ibrahim Khan was also doing his utmost to resolve the various issues.

On 25 September 1857, General Outram arrived with reinforcements, fought his way past the Hindustani army and entered the Residency. Sharafuddaula was in Qaiserbagh and engaged with the British in bloody combat. He took a bullet to the shoulder but eventually recovered from it.

Mahmudabad's forces were stationed near Gannay Wali Gali, and Riyaz and a few of his men had placed informants at regular intervals between Qaiserbagh and Gannay Wali Gali. No sooner had General Outram entered the Residency, than Raja Nawab Ali Khan arrived with his troops from Baari★ and surrounded it.

Risaldar Syed Barkat Ahmad Qasim Khan tried to enter the Residency with his troops but came into the line of fire of his own cannons and had to retreat. After three days, Raja Nawab Ali Khan retreated to Baari and wrote a letter to Maulvi Ahmadullah Shah saying that British spies had reached Kanpur and Allahabad and that, in order to stop them, forces should be stationed outside the city.

Maulvi Ahmadullah Shah had foreseen this, and immediately dispatched Riyaz to see Raja Beni Madhao of District Purwa. Raja Beni Madhao's forces were stationed at regular intervals between Rae Bareilly and Unnao. As he showed Riyaz a contingent of men in Mangal Dara†, Raja Sahib said to Riyaz, 'If Bhagwan has written defeat for us,

---

★ Baari was a place between Sitapur and Lucknow near Sidhauli where Raja Nawab Ali Khan had stationed his troops and set up camp. The camp became key to the resistance particularly as people from the north would arrive there and be given some basic training before being sent off to fight in Lucknow. This was the place where either at the end of March or in the first week of April there was a bloody engagement between the troops of Maulvi Ahmadullah Shah and Brigadier Hope Grant. (*Sitapur Gazetteer* contains complete details.)

† Mangal Dara was a cantonment in district Purwa on the Lucknow road. In its place today, stands the Magarwara railway station that falls between Unnao and Kanpur.

then we can do nothing but I can tell you one thing: no firangi will pass us here, we will fight to the last man.'

Riyaz returned from Purwa on the eighth day and presented his eyewitness reports before the War Council. General Bakht Khan said to Riyaz, 'I have reliable information that an English general, Colin Campbell, has avoided Raja Beni Madhao's forces and found an alternative way to Lucknow. I have also got news that General Hope Grant is advancing.'

General Bakht Khan's spies were right. On 13 November 1857, General Colin Campbell fought his way through Hindustani forces and arrived at Alam Bagh in Lucknow. Maulvi Ahmadullah Shah brought this to the notice of the War Council and, arguing for action, said, 'We should have a decisive battle with the British in Alam Bagh.'

Risaldar Syed Barkat Ahmad Qasim Khan, Raja Jai Lal Singh and the Thakurs of Nagram all supported his decision. Other officers also agreed with this plan of action but before they were able to attack Alam Bagh, Campbell attacked and captured Dilkusha as well as La Martinière.

Risaldar Barkat Ahmad immediately took up positions in Sikander Bagh, and the next day 3000 men put their lives on the line to defend their cause. Campbell's army had 9000 well-armed Gurkhas and Sikhs, supported by naval cannons patrolling the river. This tactical and numerical advantage meant that 3000 Hindustanis were massacred by nightfall. The next day the firangis captured Shah Najaf, Moti Mahal, Khursheed Manzil, Taare Wali Kothi and Chattar Manzil. They cleared a path all the way to the Residency and, under the protection of artillery fire, they escorted the women

and children out of the Residency and took them to Alam
Bagh.

Seeing this deteriorating situation, Maulvi Ahmadullah
Shah attacked the British with ferocity, pushing them out of
the city. He wanted to attack Alam Bagh and Dilkusha but
did not have enough ammunition, so he sent runners in all
directions to ask for reinforcements.

Raja Nawab Ali Khan sent six loads of ammunition
and others also sent help from Nawab Ganj, Purwa,
Daryabad and other places, including fresh battle-ready
soldiers. However, by the time they arrived, the British
had reinforced their position. The Hindustanis surrounded
both places from all sides and their siege became tighter and
tighter as the days passed.

The British had already taken back Delhi and enlisted
36,000 men from Punjab and Afghanistan and were
marching on Lucknow.

Maulvi Ahmadullah Shah made the siege fiercer and
prepared for the oncoming forces. He informed the War
Council of the developments and, taking command of the
army, asked General Bakht Khan to station his forces near
Chakkar Wali Kothi. He also informed Raja Nawab Ali
Khan and together they ensured that troops were placed all
around Lucknow. Riyaz, accompanied by a cavalry of 200
men, patrolled the entire city. Every child from Basheerat
Ganj to Nawab Ganj, all the way to Baari was familiar with
Riyaz, and wherever he arrived, people would mob him.

Sharafuddaula the Second, Ghulam Reza Khan was
in charge of civil supplies and his close aide Umrao Mirza
had accompanied Riyaz on his patrols. They sent supplies

from wherever they could. In the last week of February 1858, a large contingent of firangis set off towards Lucknow from Kanpur. Raja Beni Madhao prevented this force from advancing, engaging them on the banks of the Ganga. However, this was a temporary victory.

The English placed their long-range cannons at the head of their columns, slowly making a path for themselves all the way to Basheerat Ganj. As the farmers saw the tide changing, they stopped sending supplies to Lucknow. Ghulam Reza Khan informed Maulvi Sahib about this. Maulvi Sahib allotted 500 men to him so they could protect the supply trains.

Ghulam Reza Khan bought Rs 15,000 worth of supplies from his personal funds and had them stored in the Nagine Wali Baradari in Qaiserbagh and also in various depots around the city. He asked Sharafuddaula Mohammad Ibrahim Khan to announce that people should stock up on supplies as soon as possible.

The news of the English's arrival had caused worry in the city but instead of running, many people chose to arm themselves in order to fight. Swordsmiths and gunsmiths were working day and night to make swords, guns and cast cannons, and others were busy making ammunition. The Hindustani armies were training new volunteers for combat.

On 6 March 1858, the English forces attacked General Bakht Khan but the Hindustani army had been deployed in such a manner that the English had to fall back to reorganize their ranks.

General Bakht Khan took advantage of this and signalled to the Kurmis of Nagram and the Afridi Pathans of Malihabad, who rushed into the ranks of the Gurkhas, Sikhs and English causing mayhem. Bakht Khan made the rest of his forces advance but, at that moment, English reinforcements from Shahjahanpur arrived, changing everything. Sharafuddaula Mohammad Ibrahim Khan also arrived with more troops and a bloody battle ensued near Maahnagar. The Hindustani armies managed to push back the English and their mercenaries, making them retreat to Kukrail.

Sharafuddaula Mohammad Ibrahim Khan was fighting from atop his elephant when a cannonball exploded near the animal, making it run amok. The elephant trampled one of his officers and Sharafuddaula turned it around and headed back towards the city. Seeing him, his troops also decided to turn and leave but Bakht Khan had the presence of mind to rally the troops, pushing back the English.

The fighting had started in Alam Bagh. Maulvi Sahib had sent fresh troops to both the battlefronts but the English forces never seemed to diminish. They were like a constant tide of uniforms pouring through an opening. Maulvi Sahib tried everything to dam this flood of soldiers, rallying troops and pushing the English assault back. Despite his best efforts, the English captured the eastern part of the city on 16 March 1858.

Seeing the impending mayhem, Birjees Qadr's mother, Begum Hazrat Mahal,★ bade her final farewell to her palace,

---

★ Begum Hazrat Mahal was one of Lucknow's most beautiful courtesans with an enchanting voice. Wajid Ali Shah fell in love with her and when he married her, he gave her the title Hazrat Mahal. She used to love a man called Mammoo Khan and he used to secretly visit her. She was Birjees

Farhat Afza,★ and left on foot with her companions. They made their way to Teela Shah Jaleel and Maulvi Ganj. Her companions dispersed and she went to Reza Ali Khan's house. Reza Ali Khan was perspicacious and knew that the English would arrive sooner or later, so he sent her to the house of Sharafuddaula Mohammad Ibrahim Khan.

Sharafuddaula lived near Sarai Ma'ali Khan. Hazrat Mahal, Birjees Qadr, Mammoo Khan and their servants and ladies-in-waiting stayed there for a night and, the next day, they returned to the house of Reza Ali Khan. The English had entered the city and there was fighting in every alley. They sent word through Kotwal Reza Ali Baig that if Begum Hazrat Mahal stayed in the city, then they would offer her protection and give her a Rs 25,000 monthly allowance. Mammoo Khan retorted to the kotwal, 'Ama Mian, are you naive? These firangs can't be trusted. No! Can't be trusted in word or deed.'

'How is one meant to reach a settlement?' Reza Ali Baig asked. 'The English say we are not going to punish ordinary people and the mutineers will simply be exiled from the city.'

'I don't trust such promises,' Mammoo Khan shot back. 'If they swear by the Bible and send a letter with the

---

Qadr's mother and on his birth, her stature increased. After Lucknow was recaptured by the British, she left for Nepal where she lived out the rest of her days.

★ Between Qaiserbagh and the Chaulakhi Gate there was a beautiful palace called Farhat Afza which is where Hazrat Mahal stayed. The palace stretched all the way to Ghasyaari Mandi. In its place today, Nishaat Talkeez and other buildings have come up.

signatures of the Khedive of Egypt and the Sultan of Rome, then maybe I shall consider their offer.'

'What a joke! As if the Sultan and the Khedive will come to India especially to a sign a letter for you!' replied Reza Ali Baig.

Without a thought, Mammoo Khan retorted, 'Well, Jung Bahadur★ is here, why don't they get him to sign?'

'Look, they are the victors and they will dictate terms! You can't have a say in that.'

Mammoo Khan turned around and tersely replied, 'Well, of course you will advocate their cause . . . '

Offended, Reza Ali Baig left.

Hazrat Mahal and Birjees Qadr would spend the day at the house of Nawab Ashrafuddaula and, come evening, go to the house which Maulvi Ahmadullah Shah had made his headquarters. The English were slowly taking over the entire city. Maulvi Ahmadullah Shah mustered his troops for a final battle but when he failed to push back the English, he retreated to Musa Bagh. Hazrat Mahal, Birjees Qadr and Mammoo Khan also joined them there.

Riyaz sought out Maulvi Sahib when he arrived in Musa Bagh.

'We have 5000 men in Baari. If you can hold this position for two days and engage the English, I will attack Lucknow while their flank is exposed.'

'Now is not the time for that,' replied Maulvi Sahib. 'You must return to your Raja Sahib. Leave immediately via Gau Ghat and Ghaila so that you reach Baari safely.

★ The Maharaja of Nepal who aided the British in quelling the uprising.

Tell Raja Sahib that he should come and escort Begum Hazrat Mahal and her unfortunate son to safety in Nepal.'

Riyaz found one of the fastest Kathiawari★ horses and, by the afternoon, he reached Baari. By the evening, Raja Sahib set off with a force of 4000 men and reached Musa Bagh. The English had already surrounded Musa Bagh but Riyaz managed to make his way to Maulvi Sahib. Under cover of the night, they escorted Begum Hazrat Mahal and her companions to the other side of the river where Raja Nawab Ali Khan was waiting with his army.

The English attacked at dawn the next day and the Hindustanis managed to kill about 2000 of them. However, the English had superiority in numbers and slowly, Maulvi Sahib retreated towards the river and eventually had to cross it.

Spies had informed their foreign masters that Birjees Qadr had left the night before and was being escorted towards Nepal by Raja Nawab Ali Khan of Mahmudabad. Hope Grant and his forces immediately set off in hot pursuit. Maulvi Sahib also had spies who informed him of this, so he set off in order to catch up and join forces with Raja Nawab Ali Khan.

'Why don't you march double time and escort Aalia Hazrat† to safety? I recommend you take 1000 men and leave the rest here with me.'

Raja Sahib left immediately with Birjees Qadr's convoy. As they left, Hope Grant's galloping force appeared on the

---

★ Translator's note: A special breed of horse from the Kathiawar region in Rajasthan that was famous for its resilience and strength.

† Translator's note: Hazrat Mahal.

horizon. Maulvi Sahib's men hid in the fields and ambushed them. In the ensuing commotion, Maulvi Sahib pushed his artillery to the front and started shelling Grant's forces.

The English retreated to the city and Maulvi Sahib gave chase, eventually entering the city once more. Yet again there was fighting in the alleys and roads. Maulvi Ahmadullah Shah made the Dargah of Hazrat-e Abbas his base and rallied the people of the city and his own men for a final attack to push out the English. However, Sikh and English reinforcements had arrived from Kanpur and Allahabad and Hope Grant tried to surround Maulvi Sahib's position. As a last resort, he had to leave the city yet again to avoid the onslaught by the Sikhs, Gurkhas and whities.

Riyaz had been fighting alongside Maulvi Ahmadullah Shah. Once they reached Mohibullahpur, he turned to Maulvi Sahib and said, 'There is no point in waiting here to engage the firangs again. If you think it appropriate, we could head towards Baari where there are still a few thousand men ready to fight.'

'I haven't lost hope, Riyaz Mian,' replied Maulvi Sahib. 'The English too are weary of fighting and if they didn't have the support of the Sikhs and Gurkhas, we would have no trouble defeating them. By now we could have flown Bahadur Shah Zafar's flag from Fort William.'

'We have sacrificed thousands of our finest men,' said one of Raja Loni Singh's officers, 'and their blood has not been spilt in vain. Drops of it will water the spirit of resistance among our people.'

'Yes, sacrifices are never in vain, though sometimes the results are not obvious.'

Maulvi Sahib had the bugle blown, so the march could begin again. The men were exhausted and could not muster the courage to take another step. They also knew that if they remained near Lucknow they could be attacked at any time by the English. They supported each other and, by nine o'clock, reached Baari.

The field, which had 8000 camps a fortnight earlier, now had barely 200. As the men stationed in Baari saw Maulvi Sahib's troops, their faces lit up and they walked out to embrace their companions.

Riyaz recognized one of the young Thakurs from Mahmudabad and asked him, 'Where did everyone go?'

'They left for their villages and said that if they were needed, they could be sent for.'

Jawahar Singh's younger brother was there. He recognized Riyaz and said, 'My brother left with Raja Sahib and first went to Mahmudabad. He then went alone from there to Sitapur. Your parents are in Mankapur.'

'Where is Miss Baba?'

'She's also there. Four or five firangi women were there the other day, but I think they have all left for Lucknow.'

'How do you know?' asked Riyaz.

'I went to Mahmudabad yesterday and returned only today.'

'Who do you camp with?'

The young man pointed towards a big tent under a bargad tree. 'We are camped over there.'

Riyaz promised to meet him again and went to talk to Maulvi Sahib to inform him about the developments. Maulvi Sahib stared into the distance as he listened, slowly turned and said, 'I spoke to the commander here. Raja Sahib has ordered these men to join forces with us. I have also given them the order to get ready. I have just got news that Hope Grant will head in this direction with a large contingent of men and will be here either tomorrow or day after. He wants to have a final battle and end this.'

Riyaz nodded, leaned over, whispered something in his ear, said 'Khuda hafiz' and walked towards the bargad tree.

15

The Advance of Hope Grant

Riyaz and a few of the young officers from Mahmudabad's army fanned out and recruited 2000 armed men over the course of a week. Some of these men had returned from fighting in Lucknow. They all collected in Baari. Maulvi Sahib's spies were informing him of the developments. The brave and fearless Raja of Ramnagar Dhamedi, Raja Guru Bakhsh Singh, had stationed his men near the Ghaghra River and was regularly in touch with Maulvi Sahib via special messengers. By the end of March, 1500 men from Ramnagar Dhamedi had joined the men in Baari.

Maulvi Sahib only had six cannons left and his ammunition was running low. He decided to put some guns on top of ravines and others on small hillocks so that he could face General Grant's army. Riyaz reached Mankapur and advised his parents and Alice to go back to Mahmudabad for a few days. Riyaz's father called Pandey Ji and asked for his advice. Pandey Ji replied,

'Riyaz, my son, do you think that the firangis won't go to Mahmudabad?'

Before Riyaz could reply, Rustam Ali Khan piped up, 'Of course they will. Raja Sahib has been one of the leaders of the uprising and was one of the first people to declare war against the British.'

'Yes, Khan Sahib. Lawrence had offered him Rs 5000 annually to not fight but he declined and his forces were at the forefront of the attack against the Residency.'

'Then why don't you go to Nana's house in Shahjahanpur?' asked Riyaz.

'No, Mian. The God who will protect us there will protect us here,' replied Rustam Ali Khan gravely. 'I am not afraid of death, only of God.'

Pandey Ji turned to Rustam Ali Khan and said, 'Khan Sahib, don't worry. The English won't question anyone here. I have given shelter to forty or forty-two Englishmen and women, and escorted many of them to Lucknow.'

Rustam Ali Khan nodded, 'Yes, Pandey Ji, I will stay here with you and if need be, I shall pick up a weapon again after five years of laying down my arms.'

Riyaz stayed with his parents in Mankapur that night. He spoke to Alice until late into the night. In the morning, he got up before sunrise and was about to leave when his mother said, 'Never turn your back on the battlefield, son. You are our pride and joy. Look after yourself and make your homeland proud of you.'

'Amma, I have never questioned orders or wavered in my resolve. I . . .'

Rustam Ali Khan interrupted, 'Whoever follows the truth, God becomes his guide.'

'The sad thing is that, despite our best efforts, nothing has worked. Anyway, I shall try until my dying breath.'

'May God keep your resolve strong and your intentions pure,' Rustam Ali Khan said with tears in his eyes as he put his hand on his son's shoulder. 'Go! Your companions will be waiting for you. Go!'

Riyaz mounted his horse and glanced towards Alice. With a quivering voice, she said, 'Riyaz, don't forget me! I don't have anyone else in this world.'

Riyaz didn't say anything, offered his salaam and rode off. As soon as he was out of sight, Alice clung to his mother and started sobbing.

'No, no, my daughter, don't cry. We should all pray that just as we saw his back we will soon see his face. I too have sent off my young son whom I have nurtured for twenty-two years. God will be kind. I know it.'

Riyaz's mother was overcome with emotion and she couldn't say another word. She just lifted her dupatta and covered her face with it.

Riyaz reached Baari early in the morning. Maulvi Sahib was astride his horse and was about to go and inspect the troops. Riyaz went up to him to offer his salaams. As their conversation continued, about eight young men gathered around them. By the afternoon, Jawahar Singh, Ramzan Khan, Laxman Pandey and Maulvi Karamat Ali had arrived, along with 300 armed men.

Before sunset, some spies returned and informed everyone that Hope Grant, along with 7000 Gurkha, Sikh

and gora soldiers, was on his way, accompanied by an artillery unit from Allahabad. By nightfall, some reconnaissance troops arrived in Baari and found out that Maulvi Sahib had set up camp nearby. Before dawn, these troops were pushed backed by Maulvi Sahib's soldiers. Maulvi Sahib and his deputies thought that Grant would attack at any time, putting his cannons at the forefront, but the English had set up camp two miles to the south.

In the evening, Riyaz sought out Maulvi Sahib and said, 'The English not attacking must mean something.'

'More than their bravery they value their cunning and tactics. I heard this sentence in Faizabad,' Maulvi Sahib replied.

'They must have their men among our soldiers,' Riyaz wondered aloud.

'Only God can know that.'

Riyaz repeated his fear to Jawahar Singh and Laxman Pandey. Halfway through the night his worries were proven true. Jawahar Singh came to his tent and woke him up.

'You won't believe what has happened, Riyaz Bhaiyya. The Balrampur lads have managed to persuade the boys from Gonda and Bahraich to desert us and almost 2000 people have left. The men from Khiri and Muhammadi are also getting ready to leave.'

Riyaz quickly put on his uniform, picked up his rifle and rushed to Maulvi Sahib's camp. He had just finished his *tahajjud* prayers★ and was about to get up from his prayer mat. They explained the situation to him and Riyaz asked, 'What should we do? Tell us, what are your orders?'

★ Translator's note: Prayers that are read in the middle of the night, a few hours before dawn.

'What is your opinion, Riyaz Mian?' Maulvi Sahib countered.

'I will fight until my last breath.'

'The battle will be bloody but let those who wish to leave, leave. They will only hamper us during the fighting. We will fight the firangs with what we have.'

Riyaz left and returned to his own tent. He was completely unnerved.

The next morning, at eight o'clock, another 1500 men deserted them. Only 5000 men remained in Baari. In the afternoon, Maulvi Sahib dispatched 1800 men to Mahmudabad and, with the remaining 3000, he faced the English. The English had forces of over 10,000. Despite this, they were not able to move forward for two days. They were about to retreat towards Lucknow when they got reinforcements. Hope Grant tried to surround the Hindustanis.

Maulvi Sahib directed his forces towards a weak flank and, fighting his way through the English army, he took his forces and made for cover. Hope Grant wanted to give chase but his soldiers were in disarray and they lost valuable time. By the evening, they were able to organize themselves into ranks again. The wounded were treated and sent to Lucknow while the dead were buried.

Maulvi Sahib had managed to reach Mahmudabad. The naazim of Sitapur, Bakhshi Har Parshad, also reached Mahmudabad at the same time. Maulvi Sahib inspected the 300-strong force that Raja Nawab Ali Khan had left in Mahmudabad.

At night, he sent for Bakhshi Har Parshad and they discussed the developments. Bakhhsi Har Parshad said,

'I have left scouts from here to Baari and it seems that it will take Hope Grant four days to reach. If you want to push him back, ambush him away from the city.'

'No,' replied Maulvi Sahib ponderously, 'the people of this area have made too many sacrifices. From Nawab Ganj to Lucknow and from Lucknow to here, Mahmudabad's army has been steadfast in its support and has gone through thick and thin with me. Raja Nawab Ali Khan is among the leaders of the Independence movement and has never faltered. He spurned the firangi's offers and has gone to escort Aalia Hazrat to Bondi. I want to prevent any more bloodshed here.'

'You're right,' said Har Parshad. 'He has been with the movement since the beginning and left all his comfort and safety to fight alongside his countrymen. Even the younger members of his family are fighting.'

'I will leave Mahmudabad in the morning,' Maulvi Sahib said stoically, 'and I swear that I will not let the firangis rest until the last drop of blood in my body remains.'

'I have heard that troops are being sent in every direction from Lucknow,' said Har Parshad. 'What are your orders for me?'

'You should make for Muhammadi. Some would say the situation looks bleak, but I have not lost hope yet.'

'What are your orders about the Qila?' asked Har Parshad.

'Empty it. The firangis will definitely shell it when they arrive.'

Riyaz was sitting silently near Maulvi Sahib. He leaned forward and said, 'I think that you should give orders to vacate the town otherwise who knows what will happen when the looting starts!'

'You will have to do this. I will leave in the morning,' replied Maulvi Sahib, 'and you can follow later.'

Har Parshad left for Sitapur. Maulvi Sahib's camp was abuzz about what might happen and in the morning, they were given their marching orders. Riyaz went from mohallah to mohallah persuading people to leave for the countryside. In the afternoon, he rested for two hours before leaving Mahmudabad himself.

Maulvi Sahib had set up camp near a small lake between Sitapur and Muhammadi and sent scouts in all four directions. Riyaz arrived after nightfall, pitched his camp and fell asleep. In the morning, he presented himself to Maulvi Sahib. Maulvi Sahib heard him intently and said, 'You and your men should stay in this area. You know it well. Set up camp in the bamboo jungles.'

Riyaz nodded.

'Keep scouting for information and send men to update me about the firangis' movements.'

'We need a hundred men for this.'

'You select them and ride by the afternoon,' said Maulvi Sahib. 'Shahjahanpur and its surrounding areas will become battlefields! I am still hopeful that our sacrifices will not be in vain.'

'Have we not been able to get any information about Raja Sahib's whereabouts?' asked Riyaz.

'He hasn't reached Bondi yet,' replied Maulvi Sahib. 'Assemble 100 men from your area and when the time is right, hit the British supply trains and put together a larger fighting force.'

Jawahar Singh was also sitting behind Riyaz. He leaned forward and asked, 'Where will we get the magazine from?'

'From Sidhauli,' Maulvi Sahib fired back. 'The ammunition has been moved there from Sitapur. Your expenses will be met by Bakhshi Har Parshad and you will not face any trouble.'

After talking to Maulvi Sahib, Riyaz and Jawahar Singh left the tent and, by the afternoon, had gathered 100 men and set off for Sitapur. Some old friends of his were in the troop. After having travelled for a few miles, Laxman Pandey turned to Riyaz and said, 'Riyaz Bhaiyya, we can stay with great comfort in the shade of the trees on the bank of the Sarayan.'

'Maulvi Karamat Ali had also advised this as we were leaving. We will keep getting supplies from Sitapur and Mahmudabad and will be able to continue to watch the movements of the English spies and troops.'

By dusk, they arrived at the banks of the river and since they knew every inch of the area, they found a suitable spot in the woods to pitch camp. The next day, using branches and small felled tree trunks, they made temporary shelters. Laxman Pandey had left for Sitapur at daybreak and returned to the camp by two in the afternoon. Bakhshi Har Parshad was still there, about to leave.

A group of twelve armed men had accompanied Laxman Pandey back from Sitapur. All of them belonged to the military police unit. Riyaz constituted a small advisory council and they held a meeting. Following this, the men were dispersed in various directions and Riyaz left for Mahmudabad. Hope Grant had still not arrived. The qasbah was empty and people had already left. Riyaz spent the night there and returned to his camp the next day.

The men used to get up before daybreak, eat and only return to the camp at night. After one week, Riyaz got news that Hope Grant had arrived in Mahmudabad and blown up the fort. He had left in the direction of Bilehra. Riyaz dispatched a messenger to Maulvi Ahmadullah Shah with the news. He had entered the precinct of Shahjahanpur and Thakur Narpat Singh had prepared his troops near Mallanvan to fight the English.

The angrez had sent their troops towards Hardoi and Sandila where they had engaged with Maulvi Ahmadullah Shah and the local taluqdar's soldiers and moved on towards Mallanvan, Shahabad and Shahjahanpur. Bakhshi Har Parshad had left Sitapur but the angrez had still not arrived there.

Meanwhile, Riyaz had reached Mankapur and went to consult his father and Ram Tirath Pandey. He was accompanied by Jawahar Singh and Ramzan Khan. Jawahar Singh was adamant that they head for Sitapur, gather new forces and continue the fight.

Riyaz's father said, 'Maulvi Ahmadullah Shah is the de facto commander of the Indian armies of Awadh. His troops are fighting the angrez virtually everywhere and I don't think you should do anything without his permission. He has eyes everywhere.'

After their conversation, Riyaz went to see his mother. When he entered the house, Alice said, 'Can I say something?'

'Yes, yes, of course.'

'I am not speaking as an Englishwoman but as someone who cares for you and for your people's future. Fate is not with you. You have not left any stone unturned in your quest for freedom but the English power is at its height and they are becoming stronger by the day.' She paused, hesitating, and continued, 'If you are willing to take my advice, I will offer it . . .'

'I know your people are getting stronger . . .'

'Don't think of me as one of them,' interjected Alice. 'If I wanted to live among them, why would I have left? Have you not even understood me this much?'

'Arré, please forgive me, Alice,' Riyaz replied, embarrassed. 'What I was trying to say is that I know that the angrez are becoming more powerful and reinforcements are coming in every day but despite this, we will continue the fight.'

Riyaz's mother interrupted, 'If you know that nothing will come of this fighting, then why continue the bloodshed? If you really believe you can win, continue the fight.'

'We cannot turn back from this fight until and unless Maulvi Sahib gives the orders.'

'The English will have to leave one day,' replied Alice. 'Wherever there are dedicated and principled young men like you, people will not remain slaves.'

Riyaz ate dinner with his mother, sisters, Alice and his brothers and, after an hour or so, set off again. He bumped into a rider from his troop somewhere near Khairabad.

The rider said, 'Raja Sahib had gone to Bondi to escort Begum Hazrat Mahal and is on his way back but is still far off. He doesn't even know that the Fort of Mahmudabad has been shelled into the ground.'

'Any other news?' asked Riyaz.

'Sultan Singh has arrested two English messengers. They were on their way to Balrampur.'

'Where are they?'

'They have been taken to your camp,' replied the rider.

Riyaz and his men rode towards Sitapur. Once they reached, their men informed them that the English had dispatched a company of Gurkhas towards Sitapur, accompanied by officers and British bureaucrats.

This was crucial news. Riyaz rode for his camp and dispatched a message for Maulvi Sahib. On the fourth day, the rider came back with a letter in which Maulvi Sahib wrote that he was waiting for Raja Nawab Ali Khan and would make a decision after consulting him. He also mentioned the situation in Shahjahanpur where Pathan soldiers were fighting the English who were holed up in a house in the centre of town. He wrote that he was trying to get them to leave the house but to no avail.

Riyaz called for a meeting with some of his friends and left for Sitapur immediately afterwards.

16

The Wisdom of
Maulvi Ahmadullah Shah

As soon as Riyaz heard about Raja Nawab Ali Khan's return, he left to meet him in Chattauni, not far from Mahmudabad. Raja Sahib hugged him and asked him about the situation in the rest of the province. Tents had been pitched for him and his family and he sat talking to Riyaz for quite some time. He heard about the destruction of the fort in Mahmudabad, and his face fell. He took a deep breath, gazed into the distance seemingly lost in thought, but determined, as if he was trying to fix his mind on something.

Riyaz said to him reassuringly, 'Sarkar, please don't worry. You are our leader and we are with you until our last breath, until they separate our heads from our bodies.'

'Riyaz . . .' replied Raja Sahib with sadness in his eyes, 'it does not bode well for us. We kept them under siege for three months and yet they were able to use cannons to blow up the Qila.'

'Sarkar, Maulvi Sahib deliberately did not engage with them in Mahmudabad; he wanted to save the people of the qasbah. He was busy fighting in Shahjahanpur at the time.'

'I know, Riyaz, I trust Maulvi Sahib and his farsightedness. He was bound by circumstance but still, it is no small feat for them to break the siege and come all the way to my Qila to destroy it.'

Riyaz nervously looked around. Raja Sahib turned to him and said, 'Go now. Let me think for a while but remain near my tent.'

Riyaz got up, bowed and left. Nearby, under the shade of a tree, his men and officers from Raja Sahib's army were busy talking to each other. Everyone knew about the destruction of the fort in Mahmudabad, their voices were subdued and their faces betrayed their grief. Every one of them, each officer and each soldier, had demonstrated their courage fighting in Lucknow.

After an hour, Raja Sahib called for Riyaz and asked about Maulvi Sahib.

Riyaz replied, 'Nawab Ghulam Qadir Khan⋆ had taken over the administration of Shahjahanpur but his forces had a direct clash with the enemy near Pachuria. Nizam Qadir Ali

---

⋆ Nawab Ghulam Qadir Khan was from the family of the Nawabs. When fighting with the English broke out and they were being killed in their bungalows, in the cantonment and other areas, Ghulam Qadir Khan became the de facto Nawab and acquired a letter from the Nawab of Bareilly accepting him as the [naazim] administrator of the city. He took over his duties but up until then Nawab Qadir Ali Khan was the naazim because the Indian forces had given him control of Shahjahanpur. Nawab Ghulam Qadir Khan's forces engaged with the British near Pachuria on 28 April 1857.

Khan was commanding Nawab Sahib's forces. The warriors fought relentlessly and pushed back the British a number of times. The British won and Nizam Qadir Ali Khan was martyred in battle. Har Parshad and others had fought courageously and eventually Nawab Sahib along with his family and retinue disappeared into the countryside.'

'What's the situation right now?' asked Raja Sahib.

'Maulvi Sahib has taken control of the situation and Bakht Khan, Firoz Shah and Ismail Khan have also reached there from Fatehgarh. Eight to ten days ago, the English had advanced and Maulvi Sahib had retreated from the town but now he has them surrounded. The English and their soldiers are besieged in the old prisons and are fighting from there.'

'Riyaz, you know that we have all accepted him as our commander,' Raja Sahib said in a calm voice, 'which is why we must set off to help him today.'

'But Sarkar, you have already travelled a long distance today.'

'Take some well-rested soldiers with you. It's not as if this fight for independence will not continue without me. There are 4500 infantry and cavalry here. Just leave 500 here and march with the remaining 4000 towards Shahjahanpur.'

Riyaz came out of the tent and spent some time talking to his colleagues. By 4 p.m., he had 4000 men ready to march for Shahjahanpur. They rested that night and were about to leave the next morning when four riders were spotted galloping in from the south-east. From their uniforms, Riyaz recognized them as Raja Sahib's personal bodyguards.

As soon as the first rider was within earshot of Riyaz, he screamed, 'Sarkar has left us!'

'Sarkar . . .?'

As soon as Riyaz said this, the word went around the ranks of the men like musket fire. Suddenly, 4000 men fell quiet. Their beloved ruler whom they had just escorted the previous day had left his earthly abode. The riders dismounted near Riyaz and before they could say anything, he said, 'From God we come and to God we shall return.'

'Sarkar has left us orphaned,' one of the riders said, trying to catch his breath. He knelt down and broke into tears.

Laxman Pandey started beating his head and the sound of men weeping emerged from all sides. Riyaz stood stock-still and, with tears glistening in his bloodshot eyes, he looked from one side to the other as if in search of something. He was not able to understand what had happened and what the riders were saying.

The rider took out a piece of paper from his pocket and stuttering, said, 'This was the last thing written by Sarkar. It's for you.'

Riyaz slowly raised his hands, took the piece of paper and unfolded it. He wiped his eyes and peered into the paper.

Riyaz,

Go and help Maulvi Sahib and fight for our freedom until your last breath.

—Nawab Ali Khan

Riyaz read the message again and, as his eyes glistened, he turned to the light. He folded the paper, put it in his pocket, turned to his men and in a loud voice said, 'Our fight for freedom continues!'

Hearing his voice, all the men stood up and shouted in unison, 'The fight for freedom must continue. It will continue. It will continue.'

Laxman Pandey dried his eyes, turned to one of the riders and asked, 'Faiyyaz Khan, tell us something at least?'

'Sarkar was already injured and he didn't show this to all of you. Last night he succumbed to his injuries.'

Riyaz discussed some more details with the riders and sent them back. He mounted his horse and inspected the ranks. The bugle was sounded and they marched off. They reached Shahjahanpur the next day.

Maulvi Ahmadullah Shah's bravery, courage and resilience had pushed back the English and people were coming to join his army from all directions. Colonel Hill★ and his soldiers were becoming weaker by the day.

Somehow, an English messenger broke through the siege and informed Sir Colin Campbell of the situation. He dispatched soldiers towards Shahjahanpur under the command of Brigadier John Jones. On 11 May, Maulvi Sahib attacked the English and was able to cause panic in their ranks but because of a few traitors, the English were able to hold their position. Meanwhile, Brigadier Jones entered the city from its eastern gate.

★ Maulvi Ahmadullah Shah attacked and captured the city on 3 May 1857 and Colonel Hill and his men were trapped and surrounded from all sides.

Maulvi Sahib didn't retreat and Riyaz and his men took the fight to alleyways and streets. Jones did not want to face Maulvi Sahib in the open. On 15 May, Maulvi Sahib attacked but Jones was able to hold his position because of his superior artillery. By 18 May, Sir Colin Campbell arrived with thousands of Gurkhas, Sikhs, English and Pathans but they still did not take on Maulvi Sahib face to face. More reinforcements had arrived from Kanpur for the English.

Maulvi Sahib strategically called for a retreat in order to regroup and consolidate his position. Sir Colin Campbell saw this but did not give chase. One Khan Bahadur, a collaborator, was giving chase to some troops towards Pilibhit and had taken thousands of men and twenty cannons with him. Campbell ordered him to retreat in order to reinforce his own troops. Maulvi Sahib decided that it was best not to engage and left the city.

Riyaz had advised them to retreat to Muhammadi. Campbell gave chase and they fought a pitched battle at the end of which bodies covered the entire area. Thousands of Gurkhas and Punjabis were cut down and killed. Campbell realized that he could not match Maulvi Sahib's troops by fighting at close quarters. He sent his cannons forward and began shelling Maulvi Sahib's position. The residents of Muhammadi had already left the town and Maulvi Sahib's troops fought to hold and protect every house. However, because of some traitorous taluqdars and dwindling ammunition, the English eventually overpowered Maulvi Sahib's men and began looting the houses.

Maulvi Sahib had lost more than half of his fighting men and, retreating into the woods, he gave the order to the rest of them to disperse. He kept 200 men and sent the rest away. The betrayal by some of the taluqdars and the lack of ammunition had broken his spirit. When the men had dispersed, he turned to Riyaz and said, 'Riyaz Miyan, I have kept these 200 men back for you. They are from your area and so you should take them and head towards Baari.'

'What about you?' asked Riyaz.

'All my colleagues and friends have gone, Riyaz. Nawab Ali Khan's death has left me broken. I just want to be left alone. You go . . .'

'Sarkar had asked us to fight until the very end.'

'The fight will continue as long as I live. Let me be for some time so I can think about what can be done. If I stay alive and come on to the field of battle again, you will be by my side.'

'I am worried that all our sacrifices will be in vain.'

'The seed has been sown and watered by the blood of the martyrs,' Maulvi Sahib said as if reading from a book. 'This plant will blossom. Maybe not in my lifetime. But our efforts will not go in vain and will be remembered by future generations.'

'Qibla . . .'* Riyaz said faintly.

'You must listen, brave son of Mahmudabad, you must heed my words . . .' Maulvi Sahib explained to Riyaz. 'God's covenant is never based on false hope. One day, He will grant us independence from them and we will fly the flag of free India proudly. Now go. You don't have much time.'

---

* Translator's note: Honorific used for those who are prayer leaders and religious heads.

Riyaz hesitantly left and Maulvi Sahib went underground for about twelve days to take stock of the situation. The Raja of Powayan in Shahjahanpur, Jagannath Singh, was an admirer of Maulvi Sahib and asked him to come to his fortress.

However, Jagannath Singh changed his mind after inviting Maulvi Sahib. On the morning of 5 June, Maulvi Sahib came close to the Powayan fortress alone, astride an elephant. Out of fear of the English, Jagannath had ordered the gates to be shut. Seeing this, Maulvi Sahib told the mahout to break the gate and enter the fortress. After a few knocks, the elephant dislodged the gate. Jagannath told his soldiers to fire a volley. Some of the bullets lodged themselves in Maulvi Sahib's chest and sides and this hero of the resistance and commander of the Indian rebel forces was martyred at the gates of his own countryman's fortress.

On seeing Maulvi Sahib fall, Jagannath Singh's brother cut off his head, wrapped it in a cloth and dispatched it to Shahjahanpur. The magistrate of Shahjahanpur had set up office in the tomb of Nawab Ahmad Ali Khan. He was eating lunch with a few people when Maulvi Sahib's head was shown to him. The officers with him took the head, hung it on the door leading to the complex and had the body exhumed. Maulvi Sahib had lived his life honourably with his head held high and even in death, his head was not bowed. Riyaz heard about his death on the third day and gathered 400 men with the intention of destroying Powayan's fort. However, on the way, he met his old friend Maulvi Karamat Ali who changed Riyaz's mind and accompanied him and his men towards Mankapur, where

Riyaz advised the men to go home. Only Laxman Pandey, Jawahar Singh and Ramzan Khan remained with Riyaz.

They reached Mankapur. His father and Pandey Ji embraced him and distributed alms among the poor. After two days, his companions went home. Alice was ecstatic to see him. She had completely transformed into an Indian and had opened a school in Pandey Ji's house in which, along with Riyaz's sister, she was teaching young girls.

Despite all his past efforts and struggles, the events of the past few weeks and the death of his leaders had taken a toll on Riyaz. He would sit on a cot outside his house, silently contemplating life. Alice tried her best to cheer him up and even took him to the woods to hunt for game but despite her best efforts, Riyaz remained sad and wistful.

After two months, Jawahar Singh came to him and said, 'An English deputy commissioner has come to Sitapur. He has given official certificates to dozens of men which free them from any liability of fighting in the war but when my older brother asked for one for me, he outright rejected the application.'

'Why?' Riyaz's mother asked inquisitively.

'He says my name is on a list of traitors who are to be held accountable for trying to overthrow the British government.'

'What's wrong in what he says?' Riyaz asked curtly. 'You were wrong in asking for a certificate of forgiveness.'

'Bhaiyya Riyaz, I only just found out about this,' Jawahar Singh replied. 'Why would I ask for amnesty and forgiveness? I am proud of what I have done and I did it because I wanted to. I was ready to sacrifice myself for our homeland. We didn't leave any stone unturned in trying to throw those bastards out. It is an entirely different thing that we were not successful.'

'You shouldn't go back to your village,' replied Riyaz. 'The English spies will never let you be and will eventually reach your village in search of you. Stay here. We'll see what happens.' He added confidently, 'They won't be able to catch us so easily.'

Alice turned to Riyaz and said, 'Riyaz, you are really naïve sometimes. The English have people everywhere and have reasserted their strength. Forget about what happened in the past and just live like normal peace-loving people. I promise you I will have your names removed from the list of traitors.'

'No, Alice,' Riyaz rebutted. 'How can this be? How can my friends' names remain in that register while I live a life of ease and comfort? I shall never be able to do this. Neither will I throw down my weapons, nor will I leave my friends behind by having my name removed from the list.'

Jawahar Singh spoke up, 'No, Bhaiyya. Our leaders Raja Nawab Ali Khan and Maulvi Ahmadullah Shah are examples for us to emulate. We should learn from their sacrifices.'

'Thakur,' Alice said, turning to Jawahar Singh, 'you have not understood my purpose.'

Riyaz interrupted her, 'Alice, in a nutshell, either everyone's names will be removed or nobody's will. Unless general amnesty is granted, we will gather again and conspire to continue the fight.'

'You need to be more practical and work according to the environment,' Alice tried to explain to Riyaz.

Riyaz's father, Rustam Ali Khan, also appeared and, seeing Jawahar Singh, asked for the news. Jawahar Singh gave him the update and said, 'Now the English want to arrest us.'

'It seems they still haven't learnt their lesson,' Rustam Ali Khan spat back.

'If they do not grant general amnesty, the next war will be bloodier.'

Alice asked Rustam Ali Khan, 'May I say something to you?'

'Yes, of course, beti. Say what you like.'

'Why don't you advise them to live a life of peace? Start a new life, perhaps.'

'If they do this, the spark that gave us hope for our freedom will disappear.'

'The spark cannot just be kept alive through fighting. There are a number of other ways to fight. A few thousand men cannot throw the British out; waging war should be put aside as an option.'

Rustam Ali Khan paused and said, 'Beti, you are very clever. Let me think about an answer to your proposition.'

He got up and went inside. Alice remained outside, talking to Jawahar Singh and Riyaz. After a while, Riyaz's mother called out to Alice from inside. When she had gone, Jawahar Singh leaned over towards Riyaz and asked, 'Riyaz Bhaiyya, why don't you marry her?'

'How can I do that?'

'Why? Don't you like her?'

'It's not a question of liking or disliking. You know that I rose up in rebellion and fought against the English until the very last moment. They are searching for me and when they find me, they will certainly hang me.'

'I don't think this will happen anymore,' Jawahar Singh replied earnestly.

'Treason is punishable by death,' Riyaz said emphatically. 'I know this and also that it is not certain whether I will live or die. Why should I marry her and leave her a widow at such a young age?'

'Riyaz Bhaiyya, how will this make a difference to her? Even if we are caught and hanged, Alice will still live here with your parents for the rest of her life.'

Riyaz bowed his head and Jawahar Singh also took his head into his hands. They both fell silent.

17

Alone in the Desert

The monsoon petered out and the rivers calmed down but the people's will to fight for their freedom remained as strong as ever. It was as if they were just waiting for the smallest indication from their leaders to pick up arms once again. As soon as the weather became more clement, the English army, their spies, informants and police fanned out across the countryside and once more their control was established, with even more ferociousness.

In Lucknow* (Awadh), the new chief commissioner Sir Robert Montgomery had begun passing all kinds of

---

* Lucknow had been regained by the British by March 1858 and Sir Robert Montgomery was appointed chief commissioner. In the same month, Lord Canning passed his famous declaration that all the properties of various rulers in Awadh had been taken over by the British except for the property owned by Balrampur, Badhana, Kotha, Sendi and Gopalpura. Additionally, anyone who handed in their arms would be granted amnesty except for those who had killed Englishmen. This announcement was made in March 1858 but was only gazetted a year later in April 1859.

new laws and appointing new rulers in various areas. Mr Thompson became the deputy commissioner in Sitapur where he established control through a newly recruited police force.

In the first few days of November, Ramzan Khan went to visit Riyaz and said, 'I have heard that twenty-five or thirty people were arrested in Khairabad and sent to Lucknow. Yesterday, the police had come to my village but since I had heard about their advance, I hid in a field and when they left, I came to see you.'

Just as he was finishing his sentence, Riyaz's father appeared, looking like he had seen a ghost.

'Beta, a troop of soldiers is on the way here. You must disappear now!'

'Abba, don't worry. I have known for some time that sooner or later I would have to be separated from all of you.'

Riyaz's father's eyes welled up. It was the first time that Riyaz had seen his father cry and he froze.

'Go. Go and get ready now, beta.'

Riyaz got dressed, slung his rifle on his back, picked up his two pistols, fixed his sword and put a dagger in his cummerbund. He turned to his father and said, 'Please tell Amma only once I have gone. Explain to her that she must have faith.'

Riyaz's voice started to falter as he felt the full weight of what was happening. He was unable to say anything else and so, said salaam to his father and left with Ramzan Khan. They left their basti and turned towards Sitapur. After two hours, passing Khairabad, they reached the banks of the Sarayan. Ramzan Khan said, 'Khan Sahib, this river has given us refuge once before. Whenever the enemies tried to surround us, we found sanctuary here.'

'We will remain here,' said Riyaz as he dismounted.

They walked on the bank and found a small cave hidden in the bracken. The river water was flowing serenely. A bloody storm had engulfed north India but the river remained as calm as it was before. Tens of thousands of people had been killed and hundreds of villages and towns were destroyed but this small patch of Awadh remained the same.

Riyaz paused for a moment and said to Ramzan Khan, 'Unsaddle the horses and take them to the forests. They will be able to feed themselves there. Only God can protect us now. He created us and he will provide for us.'

'I have provisions for four or five days and by then, we can try and think of something.'

'God is the sustainer,' replied Riyaz. 'Anyway, if we've put our heads in the mortar then why would we fear the pestle?'*

'Jawahar Singh and Laxman Pandey will arrive here tomorrow.'

'Did you tell them?' asked Riyaz.

'Yes. Perhaps you don't remember but when we were disbanding, I told everyone that if they felt they were in danger, they should come to this spot. I have been coming here every four days or so to check.'

They took their belongings into the cave and hid them there. They let the horses loose and went to the river to wash their hands and faces. Afterwards, they stretched out

---

* Translator's note: '*Jab oakhliyan mein sar rakha to musalon ka dar kaisa!*'

near the mouth of the cave. Riyaz hadn't slept for many days, and he immediately fell asleep. When he woke up, the sun was about to set. Ramzan Khan saw him yawn and said, 'Khan Sahib, you slept like a bear.'

'At home, I felt like a prisoner awaiting punishment. I hadn't slept for a few days recently but today I was liberated and I slept to my heart's content.' He got up, washed in the river and returned.

Ramzan Khan was sitting, lost in thought. Riyaz sat next to him. Three more of their comrades arrived by the evening from Biswan. One of them had joined the army of Narpat Singh. Riyaz asked him for an update and he said, 'The collector of Shahjahanpur is arresting men in his area and sending them to Bareilly.'

'That's what's happening here. Everywhere, sipahis and chowkidars are out looking for their comrades.'

They fell asleep that night, scattered in the caves. The next day, Jawahar Singh, Laxman Pandey and eight other men arrived. On seeing Riyaz, Jawahar Singh said, 'Thompson has put a bounty on our heads.'

Ramzan Khan got up and said, 'Khan Sahib, why don't we return the favour?'

'No!' replied Riyaz, 'we must always fight those who fight us face to face.'

'I agree, Bhaiyya,' replied Jawahar Singh. 'Anyway, no good will come of it because the English will just get more furious and search for us with even more zeal.'

During the day, Laxman Pandey put on the clothes of a farmer and went to Sitapur to buy essential provisions. When he returned, he said, 'The police have uniforms like the military and have been stationed at various points in the city.'

Jawahar Singh turned to Riyaz, 'Riyaz Bhaiyya, how long will we hide here like thieves and brigands?'

'I have been thinking about this. Don't worry, I will come up with a plan in a day or two.'

On the fourth day, they heard that an armed company of men was headed their way. By then, twenty-two men had gathered there with Riyaz and the collector had been informed of their whereabouts. As soon as they heard the news, they saddled up and rode towards Mahmudabad.

Villagers near Mahmudabad supplied them with provisions and they seemed to be all right for the time being, but the police eventually tracked them down. Riyaz's men fled and reached the banks of the Ghaghra. There were already dozens of men who had fought in the war seeking shelter there and new groups continued to arrive.

A zamindar belonging to the area of the Raja of Ramnagar Dhamedi, Thakur Manohar Singh, found Riyaz and said to him, 'Khan Sahib, how long can we survive like this?'

'God knows, Thakur Sahib.'

'If you think it wise, we can muster a force of 1000 to 1500 men.'

'Yes,' interjected Jawahar Singh, 'I too think that we should prepare for a final battle. Death in the battlefield is a thousand times better than this life.'

Riyaz paused to think and said, 'I am going and will return after one week. All of you should wait for me here.'

Riyaz shared some information with Jawahar Singh and set off. He spent the night on the banks of the Ghaghra and in the morning, was back in the saddle. He saw the new armed constabulary with their distinctive uniforms and evaded them. On the third day, he arrived in Mankapur. He called out in a hushed tone and Ram Tirath Pandey rushed out.

'Riyaz beta, are you all right?'

'I am alive, but I am also sick of this life.'

'This is what God intends,' replied Pandey. 'Don't lose hope, for victory is always with the righteous.'

He called out to Rustam Ali Khan and Riyaz went inside. His mother embraced him and started crying. Alice and his sisters also started crying. Rustam Ali Khan told everyone to be quiet and said that the police had camped in Mankapur for fifteen days waiting for Riyaz and that every few days their spies would come, but now they thought that he had gone away.

Rustam Ali Khan and Pandey Ji went to Sitapur the next day in order to see the lay of the land and found out that a new law had been instituted just after the New Year. Rustam Ali Khan said that they were not being as harsh as before in seeking out people who fought against the English. He recounted the names of some people who had sought amnesty and had not only been forgiven by Thompson but were also given a certificate saying so.

Riyaz sought counsel from his parents and Pandey Ji about what to do and they explained that continuing to fight would be pointless. Alice also tried her best to explain to him the futility of war.

She said, 'I think you should go and meet Thompson and if you don't want to, let me go and speak to him on your behalf.'

'No, Alice. I can't do anything simply out of self-interest. I would not be able to live with myself knowing that I am free but that my friends and fellow soldiers are living like homeless exiles in the wilderness. We fought shoulder to shoulder in the war and we will continue to live together.'

'I am going to go and speak to Thompson and if he doesn't listen, I will go to Robert Montgomery,' said Alice.

'Won't he take action against you?'

'No,' replied Alice, 'both my brothers have gone back to England. Thompson had someone sent here to fetch me but I told him I wanted to live here.'

Rustam Ali Khan also tried to change Riyaz's mind and, after an hour of wrangling, arguing, debating and heated exchanges, he decided that he would go to Lucknow with Alice to see Robert Montgomery.

'It's not safe for me to stay here,' said Riyaz.

'It's not,' replied Alice. 'You should go back to your companions and when we return from Lucknow, we will send word to you.'

'I'll take men from here to the Sarayan and will come back here every three or four days,' said Riyaz.

He left that night and reached his destination on the twelfth day. Meanwhile, Laxman Pandey went to see Pandey Ji, came back and told Riyaz that his father and Alice had gone to Lucknow. The informants and spies had come to the villages but had then moved on towards Khiri.

Riyaz went home to see his mother and sisters. That same day Rustam Ali Khan and Alice returned from

Lucknow and were overjoyed to see Riyaz. His mother hurried to greet them and asked, 'What news for my Riyaz?'

'Nothing has happened yet,' replied Riyaz's father. 'Alice spoke to the chief commissioner for ages in front of me and he seems like a decent man but his officers have filled his ears.'

'Will Riyaz have to live like a fugitive in the jungle? The world is getting bits of paper with amnesty and somehow Riyaz is paying for everyone else,' exclaimed Riyaz's mother.

'Amma,' Alice said, turning to Riyaz's mother, 'we tried everything. I spoke to Robert Montgomery for close to two hours in front of Abba Mian but that scoundrel Macmillan has already filled the commissioner's head.'

'Which Macmillan?' Riyaz asked. 'The same one that I gave refuge to?'

'Yes,' replied Alice, 'the one that you protected is now after your life. He even told the commissioner not to allow me to stay here. Don't worry, he won't be able to do anything. I am an adult and therefore, according to English laws, I am free to choose where I want to live.'

'Alice, don't ruin your life. If you don't want to live in Lucknow, go back to England.'

'If this will make you happy,' Alice replied, looking him directly in the eye, 'I will certainly leave.'

Her lips started trembling and her voice stuttered.

'No, I won't let you go anywhere,' Riyaz's mother exclaimed as she put her arms around Alice. 'Don't pay heed to what Riyaz is saying.'

'Alice, I am not saying this for any other reason, but how long will I be able to continue living in the shadows?

You know that they are after me. One day the spies will find me and arrest me. After that, you know as well as I do what will happen.'

Alice was crying silently and Riyaz's mother was using her dupatta to dab her eyes and wipe her face.

'Why are you crying? Riyaz didn't mean that he wants you to go. He was just telling you what he thinks the reality is, so if you wish to go to England, you can,' said Riyaz's mother.

'But why am I told this again and again?' Alice asked in a strained voice. 'When I have told you all so many times that I want to stay here with you, then why do you insist? If you really want me to go, then I will go.'

'No, Alice, this is not what I meant. All I was saying is that nothing is certain. Today I am free, tomorrow I might be arrested,' said Riyaz.

'One can't change one's fate,' replied Alice as she cleared her throat, 'but I am sure the governor-general will grant general amnesty very soon. Sir Robert is a wise, perspicacious and experienced man. It is because of him that there is a semblance of peace. Whatever difficulties remain will also subside very soon.'

They spoke to each other for a few hours, and Riyaz went to sleep. His mother woke him up for morning prayers. He ate breakfast after praying and slipped away.

One month later, Alice went back to Lucknow with Riyaz's father to meet Sir Robert. This time, Macmillan was there. He turned to Alice and said, 'Very soon, I will be made superintendent of police and will move to Sitapur.'

'This is not a duty you will be able to carry out,' Alice retorted defiantly. 'You are not worthy of working as a bookkeeper in a tavern.'

'What do you mean?' Macmillan asked angrily.

'What I mean is that you aren't fit to work with all the free alcohol available there.'

Sir Robert smiled at her reply. Macmillan took her outside and tried to explain things to her in a friendly way, but she shouted at him and made him shut up. She then went over to Riyaz's father who was pacing to and fro in the garden. They both left.

Riyaz continued to go to Mankapur every four or five days. At the beginning of the year 1859, Macmillan was made superintendent of police in Sitapur and, within a week, he started going on patrols in the area. He knew Alice lived in a place called Mankapur, so he made that his first destination. Alice used to often take a gun into the woods and bring back some game or birds to eat.

That day she had gone hunting and, as it happened, was on her way back when Macmillan saw her from a distance and spurred his horse on to catch up with her. She did not so much as look at him and made her way towards Pandey Ji's haveli.

Macmillan went towards the haveli with his soldiers and when he arrived, he called out to her. She replied, 'Macmillan, if you don't leave right away, I will inform Thompson of this. You have no right to interfere in people's lives like this.'

'I've just come to a friend to ask after her health and well-being,' replied Macmillan in a conciliatory tone.

'Thank you, but you should be out on your rounds right now so people feel secure. You shouldn't neglect your duty.'

Macmillan left straight away.

Pandey Ji asked Alice, 'What was he saying?'

'He was asking if all is well.'

'He doesn't look like he means well,' Pandey Ji said, looking into the distance. He went to drink some coconut water and Alice disappeared into the haveli.

18

The Last Proclamation

Riyaz's father had come out to sit by the chaupal when Alice came running into the haveli with a rifle in her hand. As soon as he saw her, he got worried and stood up, frantically looking in all directions while shouting out to his servant Bhullan Khan. Bhullan was sitting in the deodhi* smoking a hookah. He rushed out and went to him. Alice came up and said, 'Abbu, Pandey Chacha is coming. I saw his trap shooting down one of the roads.'

'Pandey Ji is back already? He must be bringing some important news. I hope Riyaz is all right.'

They both waited nervously as they strained to catch sight of Pandey Ji at the end of the alley which led up to the haveli. Bhullan Khan went a few steps forward and called out to someone, 'Sarju, go tell everyone that Pandey Ji is arriving.'

---

* Translator's note: Entrance to the women's section of the house.

Pandey Ji arrived on his trap. An elderly servant of his held the reins as Pandey Ji sat at the back with a long rifle, looking alert and rather pleased with himself. Seeing him happy, the expression on the faces of Riyaz's father and Alice changed and they went forward to greet him. The trap pulled into the haveli and, Pandey Ji jumped out from it like a young man and hugged Riyaz's father.

'Khan Sahib, congratulations! Our Raja has got back his state!'

'Our Raja's state?' asked Riyaz's father, bewildered. 'Our late Raja? Our Raja who died for his people?'

'Yes, Khan Sahib, yes. Kunwar Amir Hasan Khan is getting back his rightful inheritance. I saw the letter written by Thompson and stamped with official seals with my own eyes. Raja Sahib's lands were all taken because he fought against the British but, on Thompson Sahib's recommendation, the chief commissioner has released most of the lands. Some have been given to Balrampur and some of Raja Loni Singh's lands have been added to Mahmudabad.'

Alice had said her salaams to Pandey Ji and quietly listened to the conversation.

'What are you saying, Pandey Ji?' Riyaz's father asked.

'Only that which I have seen with my own eyes. I have come to fetch all of you. Eight days from now, there will be a durbar and celebrations and Thompson will go to Mahmudabad to place the crown on Kunwar Sahib's head himself and invest him with authority.'

Alice said, 'Pandey Chacha, come into the shade of the chaupal.'

'Beti, I am not going mad because of the heat. I'm telling you the truth.'

Riyaz's father took Pandey Ji into the chaupal. Bhullan fixed a hookah for Rustam Ali Khan while Sarju brought a pail and an urn with which Pandey Ji washed his hands and face. He sat on a charpoy and said to Riyaz's father.

'Khan Sahib, this is how Bhagwan fixes that which is broken.'

Rustam Ali Khan, Bhullan and Alice were all still looking at Pandey Ji in disbelief.

Pandey Ji wiped his face with his angowcha and said, 'Thompson went towards Mahmudabad about fifteen days ago on his rounds. During those days, Nawab Mohammad Khan of Farrukhabad had also gone to see Kunwar Sahib.'

'So he too stood up for friendship, did he, eh Pandey Ji?' Bhullan interjected.

Riyaz's father told him to pipe down. 'Listen to what he has to say first.'

Alice also told him to be quiet.

Pandey Ji continued, 'The Qila has been under reconstruction for the past month. Nawab Sahib was staying in a tent near the former guesthouse when Thompson showed up. His memsahib was with him and they were both riding their horses. Musahib Ali was also sitting next to Nawab Sahib. They both greeted the Englishman when Kunwar Sahib★ came outside, holding the finger of one of his

---

★ He was five or six years old at the time.

retainers. His little turban had a small *kalghi** and in his sash was a little sword. Seeing the little soldier, the memsahib got off her horse, picked up Kunwar Sahib and gave him a kiss.'

'Whoever sets eyes on Kunwar Sahib can't help but be captivated by him,' replied Riyaz's father.

'Anyway, you know Sheikh Musahib Ali. He never falters at moments such as these. As soon as he saw her pick him up, he bent down and did a *farshi salaam* and said, "Huzoor, you have taken the child into your embrace and this is a very serious gesture, for you must also live up to this affection that you have shown. This is how kings have often got their kingdoms." Thompson laughed and said, "I see, I see, this is the Raja's son. He looks very sweet."'

'Thompson is a civilized Englishman,' piped up Riyaz's father.

'He's very civilized,' agreed Pandey Ji and continued, 'After this, Nawab Mohammad Khan said to Thompson Sahib, 'Sir, this is now your child. You are responsible for him.' Thompson smiled. Nawab Sahib asked for some chairs to be brought and they all sat for some time talking among each other. When they were about to leave, the maim sahib went into the *mahalsara* and met the Rani Sahiba. She told her that this is not just your child but ours also. Someone will have to come to Sitapur regularly to let me know about his well-being.'

Riyaz's father looked up and, with a quivering voice, said, 'O Allah of all the worlds, you know that which we cannot know, please help me in my predicament.'

---

* Translator's note: *Kalghi* is a bejewelled ornament used to decorate turbans. It often also has a plume.

'Khan Sahib, don't be sad. Bhagwan will also heed your prayers.'

Riyaz's father's eyes welled up. Alice also drew in a sharp breath and turned her face away. Sarju brought some sherbet. Pandey Ji took the sherbet and said, 'Bring me a *chillum*.'★

Sarju left. Pandey Ji drank the sherbet and Alice went into the haveli. Pandey Ji turned to Riyaz's father and said, 'You need to go back to Mahmudabad today. The Rani Sahiba told Sheikh Musahib Ali that you must be brought back. The townspeople are coming back. While he was leaving, Nawab Sahib also said that he was going to leave and that he needed to send you to Lucknow to buy some important things.'

Riyaz's father went inside and told the ladies about the good news. They left Mankapur that evening and reached Mahmudabad at night. Riyaz's father went straight to the Qila to offer his salaams and, the next day, he got busy with preparations for the durbar. Nawab Sahib assured him that he would speak to Thompson about Riyaz.

Two days before the durbar, Riyaz came to see his family. His parents, sisters and Alice began crying softly when they saw him. They couldn't even raise their voices for fear of arousing the suspicions of spies and informants. Riyaz comforted them and they ate dinner and talked late into the night. Riyaz left again before daybreak.

Riyaz's mother's health was getting affected because of her worry for her son and Alice was also always lost in

---

★ Translator's note: *Chillum* is a hand-held pipe.

her own world. Despite this, she would try and joke and make light of the situation in order for them to feel better. Riyaz's father was busy with preparations for the durbar as he had been given the responsibility of decorations. He had worked hard to make Mahmudabad look like a newly-wed bride. Thompson, his officers, nearby dignitaries and other Rajas who attended the durbar praised the organization and decoration. Music was playing around the qasbah and people were hugging each other to offer congratulations.

In the late afternoon, the durbar was held on the Qila's grounds. Thompson placed the turban on Kunwar Amir Hasan Khan's head and tied a kalghi to it. The police and soldiers let out a volley to mark the occasion. Thompson read out Lord Canning's proclamation, which he had issued in March 1858 but which had only been gazetted in 1859. He also read out a proclamation written by the chief commissioner in connection with the coronation of Kunwar Amir Hasan Khan. As soon as the readings ended, cries of congratulations rippled through the crowds and offerings were made to the deputy commissioner. The durbar was called to an end just before the evening prayers.

At night, fireworks lit up the sky and a banquet was prepared which everyone partook in, from the dignitaries to the townspeople. Sweetmeats were distributed to the children.

The next day, in the presence of Thompson, a durbar was called in the name of Raja Amir Hasan Khan and the newly crowned Raja was given *nazranas*.★ During the

---

★ Translator's note: Offerings.

ceremony, Nawab Sahib asked Thompson for amnesty for Riyaz. He replied, 'Nawab Sahib, I am sorry but my hands are tied. He caused great harm to us during the war and fought against us at various fronts. A bounty has been announced for twenty-two of the leading officers from Awadh who were at the forefront of the fight and Riyaz is one of them.'

Nawab Sahib said, 'If you are able to give a child his kingdom back, surely you can get amnesty for Riyaz.'

Thompson replied, 'Raja Nawab Ali Khan raised the flag of revolt against us but he is no longer in this world and our fight is not with his family.'

Eventually, Nawab Sahib persuaded Thompson to have a word with Montgomery about Riyaz's amnesty and Alice also spoke at length to Mr and Mrs Thompson.

Riyaz was living out his days in the jungle near Khiri. He had promised Alice that he would not pick up a gun except to defend himself. Jawahar Singh, Laxman Pandey, their companions and 200 Thakurs from Ramnagar Dhamedi had also arrived in that jungle. Others who had taken part in the uprising of 1857 were also drifting in.

These young and old men had not given up their arms or given up hope. Jawahar Singh had raised a force of 800 men. They had guns that they had stolen from the British and they also had sixteen light cannons. They were getting ready to rise up and fight the British once more, but Riyaz knew that this was going to be a futile attempt. It would be like fighting a mountain. He managed to calm Jawahar Singh down.

When Jawahar Singh, Ramzan Khan and the others heard about Lord Canning's 1858 proclamation, they were

agitated and started preparing for war. Riyaz had gone
to Shahjahanpur and when he returned to find out the
intentions of his companions, he explained to them that the
British would have to revoke the proclamation one day.

The fighters had no source of provisions, so once in
a while they would go into the villages where people
would not only feed them but also send victuals back
with them.

Awadh was once more at peace and contingents of
police had been dispatched to patrol the various districts.
However, they never took on this rag-tag army and, even
if they did set out to try and encircle them, the farmers and
shepherds would alert the rebels beforehand.

Macmillan knew that these men were in the area and
that Riyaz went to meet his parents and Alice once in a
while. However, he never dared to try and capture Riyaz.
He had heard of Riyaz's legendary exploits and was afraid
of the mythic and heroic status that Riyaz had acquired
in the eyes of the people. He also knew that Alice would
never leave Riyaz's parents while he was still alive and so he
began to try and influence Thompson. When Thompson
returned to Sitapur, Macmillan said to him, 'You should
give orders for Riyaz's arrest, so that we can declare Sitapur
fully cleared.'

'But he is not disturbing the peace.'

'He is a traitor, and not only that—he is the leader of
the traitors.'

'Macmillan, you have not tried to understand the
people of this area and neither have you tried to understand
the cause of the bloody revolt.'

Macmillan didn't expect a reply like this and he continued to stare at Thompson.

Thompson went on and said, 'I know that there are thousands of rebels hidden in Sitapur, Lakhimpur, Bahraich and other places who have taken refuge near the banks of the Ghaghra and in the adjoining woods. I also know that they come out into the villages, but it's better to not prod this wasp nest! They will slowly disperse themselves. If we do take action, perhaps this time the war will be so bloody that not only will it spread in all the districts, but the native soldiers will not help us this time. It's wiser to let sleeping dogs lie.'

'Their very existence is a brazen challenge to the government. Riyaz's presence in this area is a very big danger for us.'

Thompson was well briefed and his informants kept him up-to-date on the movements of the soldiers and their leaders and even about what was happening inside the jungles. He looked Macmillan in the eye and said in an authoritative tone, 'Macmillan, it seems that you have a personal vendetta against Riyaz and don't think I don't know what the reasons are. Riyaz is single-handedly responsible for stopping another wave and for persuading his companions that fighting would be futile. It's only because of him that men like Jawahar Singh, Ramzan Khan and Gurnihal Singh have not begun attacking and looting our interests across the district. I know their presence is a danger but attacking them cannot avert this danger. I have written to Sir Robert asking him to grant a general amnesty. All of these men are from this area and we can extend a hand of friendship to them.'

Macmillan remained quiet and, when Thompson finished, he said, 'The kotwal of Sitapur Tej Narain and the subedar of the second battalion of military police, Murtaza Khan, say that they can assassinate individual rebel leaders. Just pick them off, one by one.'

'Tej Narain is spewing nonsense. A record of his so-called exploits has been sent to Lucknow and as for the bravery of Murtaza Khan, well, everyone knows the truth behind it.'

Tej Narain and Murtaza Khan had gained government posts by spying on their countrymen and had also fled the scene during battle, leaving behind arms and money collected as revenue taxes. However, they had managed to have people represent them to the chief commissioner and no action was taken against them.

Macmillan left Thompson, deflated, but began conspiring with Tej Narain and Murtaza Khan on how to kill Riyaz. An orderly in their office had fought alongside Riyaz and he would listen in on the conversations and have word sent to Riyaz through a common friend.

Meanwhile, the companions of Raja Guru Bakhsh Singh of Ramnagar Dhamedi and Thakur Narpat Singh of Mallanwan had become sick of their lives in exile and were increasingly becoming more inclined to fight. They had started gathering men on the banks of the Sarayan for one last stand and acquiring ammunition and gunpowder. They had unanimously made Riyaz their commander. Their messengers had been dispatched and were waiting for the fearsome Pathans who had fought off the English in Bareilly and Pilibhit and then gone underground in the forests.

When Riyaz realized that the English would not let him and thousands of others like him return to lives of peace, he decided that he would accept the responsibility that the others had placed on him. He went, one last time, to Mahmudabad to meet Alice and his family. His ancestral house was a haveli on the edge of the town, on the road leading to Sitapur. He reached home after nightfall. His mother leapt up to hug him and started crying, his father tried to hide his tears while his brothers and sisters also started weeping. Alice stood at a distance looking at him with longing eyes. She was wearing a light cotton shalwar qameez and a dupatta made of *tanzeb*. Seeing her standing there, looking so forlorn, Riyaz couldn't control his emotions and so he went up to her, clasped her hand and asked, 'Why are you standing alone so far away, Alice?'

Instead of replying, she looked at him intently yet wistfully, as if she wanted to say that I know I will never get close to you. Riyaz's parents could not stand the two young people's sorrow and, after a while, his father said, 'Riyaz beta, Alice's sacrifices should not be in vain. Your mother also prays and hopes for this. We both want you to marry Alice. I want you to grant us this wish today, right now.' His mother repeated the same thing while Alice stood silently, her head bowed towards the ground, weeping silently. Riyaz looked at her and lowered his head. Riyaz's father then said, 'Son, Alice has the same position among her people that you have here. She is more like our own daughter. Marriage completely changes people. Perhaps your marriage will also open doors to new possibilities. Perhaps, Insha Allah, it will be a herald for hope.'

Riyaz explained the new situation to Alice and his parents, but despite this, his father said to his mother, 'You prepare Alice for the wedding and I will go and get Maulvi Rajab Ali Sahib. You girls go and call women from the locality.' Riyaz continued to protest but it fell on deaf ears. Riyaz's brothers and sisters also began to run around carrying out preparations.

Alice was still standing next to Riyaz and, when no one else was around, she turned to him and said, 'Riyaz, why have you always remained so distant? Do you not think me worthy of being your lifelong friend and partner?'

'No, Alice, not at all,' replied Riyaz in a loving tone. 'Please don't think like this, I don't even know what to say. Only God knows what is in my heart.'

'Then why have you refused to marry me all this time?' Alice asked him with a piercing look.

'You know that they are baying for my blood, Alice, and that there is a bounty on my head. Their informers are busy trying to sniff me out. I will be arrested one day and shot. I don't . . . I don't . . . I don't want you to become a widow so young.'

'Riyaz, I am willing to give up everything for you,' Alice said in a quivering voice. 'But you should never lose faith in God.'

Riyaz's mother appeared and took her away.

Some of their relatives had arrived and some women from the neighbourhood also showed up. Riyaz's cousin sister asked him to get up and wash. Riyaz's father, his brother-in-law, his nephews and other relatives were busy with preparations outside. Riyaz had reached his house around 6 p.m. and all the preparations were done within two hours. After the *isha* prayers, Alice and Riyaz were married and, after half an hour, his mother called him into the house for some important rituals. Alice was sitting on the veranda with some girls. She was dressed in her bridal clothes and was staring at the floor intently.

Riyaz had just stepped into the courtyard when his younger brother came running in and hugged Riyaz, crying loudly. Their mother was astonished and asked him, 'Beta, is everything all right?'

'The police are outside and the officer is asking about the whereabouts of Bhai Sahib.'

Riyaz's mother shrieked out and clung to Riyaz, crying loudly. Alice got up, removed her veil and clung to Riyaz on the other side. Riyaz's sister also started weeping. Someone called out to Riyaz and he turned to his mother and Alice and said, 'One cannot fight fate. I didn't want to die like this and this is exactly why we had thought we would put up one last stand. But . . .' he took a deep breath, 'perhaps this is what God had ordained.'

Again a voice called out, 'Riyaz, Subedar Murtaza Khan and Kotwal Tej Narain Singh are waiting for you outside.' Everyone knew that these two men were baying for Riyaz's blood. Riyaz's mother fainted and some women managed to catch her. Riyaz started walking towards the deohri. Alice walked with him. Riyaz's father and his relatives were standing in the doorway.

Riyaz opened the door and his eyes fell on Murtaza Khan and Tej Narain. Behind them he could see an entire group of armed policemen. They saw Riyaz, saluted him and came forward.

They shoved a piece of paper in his direction and Tej Narain said, 'Riyaz Ahmad Khan, congratulations. You have been granted amnesty by the good grace of the British government.* This is the deed, signed, stamped and sealed. It just arrived from Lucknow today and the honourable deputy commissioner acted upon it with urgency and dispatched us straight away.'

Riyaz looked at everyone bewildered and Alice was so overcome with joy that she grabbed his arm and put her head on his shoulder without caring who was watching.

Riyaz started to read the amnesty certificate and his father embraced him and said, 'Riyaz, my beta, Riyaz, the light of my eyes.' He couldn't say anything else. The news had already spread inside and the sound of crying turned into the sounds of joy and laughter. Slowly, drums and singing filled the air in the haveli, in his neighbourhood and finally in the entire town.

The British government had revoked Lord Canning's declaration and had passed new orders granting unconditional amnesty to everyone who fought in the war. Riyaz's

---

* Mr Strachy writes that when news of Lord Canning's March 1858 proclamation reached London it was decided that it would be wiser not to punish the people of Awadh but to be more welcoming and grant amnesty to all those who fought against the British. This also meant that two-thirds of the taluqdars became close to the British and were not punished for participating in the rebellion. On 26 October 1860, a durbar was hosted by the governor-general in Lucknow in which sanads or deeds were handed out to all the attendees.

relatives surrounded him in the deohri and Alice, still in her bridal clothes, was pushed closer to him. Riyaz picked her up, went inside and, after saying prayers of thanks and finishing some more rituals, they disappeared into the bridal room.

Acknowledgements

Initially, I was hesitant to translate this novel because, as I said in my introductory essay, the reasons for doing so were personal. I am therefore grateful to my parents, Amma and Abba, and my brother, Amir, for encouraging me to do so regardless of those fears.

I am grateful to my colleagues at Ashoka University. In particular, thanks are due to Prof. Rudrangshu Mukherjee and Prof. Rita Kothari, for very generously providing blurbs for the book. Just as I was embarking on writing the introduction to this book, I found out that Dr Umair Manzar had published a book on Tarzi in December 2020. Dr Manzar was kind enough to give me a copy before it arrived at the shops, and also spent time talking to me about Khan Mahboob Tarzi and his oeuvre. The introduction would not have been possible without his help.

The late Sagheer Hasan Naqvi Sahib obtained a copy of the original 1957 edition of *Aghaaz-e-Sahar*, as the one from our library was in a bad condition. I occasionally discussed some of the sections with Nawab Husain Afsar Sahib and am thankful for his insights. Many years ago, I received a message from the Instagram page of Daak Vaak, asking whether I had a digital copy of *Aghaaz-e-Sahar*. It was serendipitous that three years later I was able to share a translated copy of the novel with Onaiza, who helped with various stylistic edits.

Kanishka Gupta was, as ever, invaluable in finding a suitable publisher. I am thankful to the patience and thoroughness of the team at Penguin Random House India, including Elizabeth Kuruvilla and Vineet Gill.

Lastly and most importantly, I am deeply grateful to Labonie Roy, who was still a student at Ashoka University when we discussed doing illustrations for this novel. As you can see, her artwork is arresting, impressive and original.

Any shortcomings in the translation are, of course, entirely mine.

                                        Ali Khan Mahmudabad